LITTLE PRINCE

THE STORY OF A
SHETLAND PONY

Annie Wedekind

Feiwel and Friends · New York

For David

(writ large!)

A FEIWEL AND FRIENDS BOOK
An Imprint of Macmillan

LITTLE PRINCE. Copyright © 2009 by Annie Wedekind.
All rights reserved. Printed in May 2009 in the United States of America
by Quebecor World, Fairfield, Pennsylvania.
For information, address
Feiwel and Friends, 175 Fifth Avenue, New York, N.Y. 10010.

Library of Congress Cataloging-in-Publication Data

Wedekind, Annie.
Little prince / Annie Wedekind. – 1st ed.
p. cm. – (Breyer horse portrait collection ; 2)
Summary: Phin, a Shetland pony, has loved leaving the carnival to
become a show pony in the big city, but when his owner loses interest in
him, he is sent to a farm for unwanted animals and must find a way
to make a home there.
ISBN: 978-0-312-38426-5
1. Shetland pony–Juvenile fiction. [1. Shetland pony–Fiction.
2. Ponies–Fiction. 3. Animals–Fiction.] I. Title.
PZ10.3.W3765Lit 2009 [Fic]–c22 2008035015

Design by Barbara Grzeslo
Feiwel and Friends logo designed by Filomena Tuosto

First Edition: 2009

10 9 8 7 6 5 4 3 2 1

www.feiwelandfriends.com

Dear Reader,

Welcome to the Breyer Horse Collection book series!

When I was a young girl, I was not able to have a horse of my own. So, while I dreamed of having my own horse one day, I read every book about horses that I could find, filled my room with Breyer model horses, and took riding lessons.

Today, I'm lucky enough to work at Breyer, a company that is known for making authentic and realistic portrait models of horse heroes, great champions, and of course, horses in literature. This beautiful new fiction series is near to my heart because it is about horses whose memorable stories will take their place alongside the horse books that I loved as a child.

This series celebrates popular horse breeds that everyone loves. In each book, you'll get to appreciate the unique characteristics of a different breed, understand their history, and experience their life through their eyes. I believe that you'll love these books as much as I do, and that the horse heroes you meet in them will be your friends for life.

Enjoy them all!

Stephanie Mazy

Stephanie Macejko
Breyer Animal Creations

CHAPTER 1

I**T'S NOT AN AVERAGE PONY THAT LIVES IN AN** apartment building. But then, Dauphin was a far from average pony—at least according to the people who groomed him, fed him, and took him for his daily constitutional in the nearby city park. He saw no reason to disagree with their judgment. His luxuriously thick coat gleamed pale gold like a freshly minted dollar coin and his cream-colored mane spilled down his neck in a rather majestic fashion (if he did think so himself). His dished face, with dark, liquid eyes peering out from beneath a rakish forelock, usually wore a pert, self-satisfied expression that suited him. If perhaps his stomach was a tad on the round side, well, he liked his oats, and there was nothing wrong with a healthy appetite . . . or with the sugar lumps, apple slices, and peeled baby carrots with which he was regularly treated.

Strictly speaking, Chadwick Ostlers, or "the Chadwick" as the stable was familiarly known, wasn't an apartment

1

building, though it was tucked in between apartment buildings (the Windsor and the Stratford) on a sunny, tree-studded block in the very nicest neighborhood in the city. With its handsome limestone facade, window boxes bursting with petunias, and impressive—though of course understated—sign (CHADWICK OSTLERS. 1886), the Chadwick was the place where the very best people boarded their horses and ponies. Inside, past the riding ring (admittedly small) and the glass viewing area (where very fit and tanned mothers perched comfortably on hunter green director's chairs, sipping chai), a ramp rose up to the second story, much in the way an elevator (or, if you were unlucky and didn't live in a building as nice as the Windsor and the Stratford, a staircase) would take you to the next floor of an apartment building. The Chadwick had four floors in all, and Dauphin's stall was at the very top, in the penthouse suite. There was only one other horse in the penthouse—an ancient, graying Friesian named Van der Luyden, who could (and often did) trace his lineage straight back to King Louis II's mount at the Battle of Mohacs. Van der Luyden's presence made the penthouse very rare air indeed . . . if a little dull.

Dauphin and his neighbor were cared for by a respectful team of grooms who took great pride in the pony they called Phin. (The only people who called the Shetland Dauphin, pronounced "doe-*fanh*," were his owner, Isabella Ingram, and her mother.) Jack, a blue-eyed, sentimental Irishman who was Phin's best friend and primary groom, was gentle but thorough with the currycomb and hoof pick. He always remembered to use the special conditioner to prevent split ends in Phin's tail, and liked to linger over their walks in the park, allowing Phin extra mouthfuls of grass or one more satisfying roll while Jack flirted with the girls who exclaimed: "What a *beautiful* pony!"

"Sure," the groom would answer. "Prettiest pony in the city!" And while an experienced fellow like Phin (he approved of the nickname, which he thought gave him a certain air) suspected that he was being used in the service of romance, he couldn't help but agree. He'd never seen a pony prettier than himself, and so he rather doubted that one existed.

· · ·

IT WAS A SPARKLING SPRING MORNING, PRO-mising the sort of spring day that poets praise and painters paint and ponies love, filled with dancing plum blossoms and dappled sunshine. The city looked freshly washed, and even the dignified faces of the limestone and brownstone buildings of Phin's neighborhood wore mellow expressions as they basked in the May sun.

The pony stood complacently in a puddle of light that spilled past the petunias into his stall, practicing great forbearance as Jack rooted around vigorously with the hoof pick. Phin knew he had to look his best today and had tolerated the buffing, polishing, stroking, and untangling that this involved without his "usual tricks." This was what Jack called his (to Phin's mind) gentle reminders of who was boss. If Jack carelessly flicked the brush over Phin's sensitive bits, or gave him a less than respectful push in order to remove a forkful of dirty bedding, it was well within Phin's rights to show Jack, with the condescension of master to servant, that he disapproved.

Here Phin's views differed from Van der Luyden's. The Friesian would probably let himself be shaved bald before murmuring the softest complaint. It was an Old World attitude that Phin found baffling. Just this morning, Jack had strolled into Van der Luyden's stall and announced in a cavalier tone: "Sorry, old sir, but I'll have to cut your brushin' short today . . . got to get your friend Phinny spick-and-span for his mistress, and if I know him and his tricks, it'll take longer than it should. Ah, but you're a gentleman and a scholar, and you understand without my explainin'." Sure enough, Van der Luyden submitted to his hasty once-over with the soft brush without even a grunt or single pinned ear. Phin would be ashamed to take such neglect without protest.

But then again, Jack never called Phin "sir" . . . or a gentleman, much less a scholar. In fact, he spoke of the pony with a good deal less reverence than anyone else did. Anyone else, that is, besides Isabella Ingram and her mother. Isabella Ingram—blond, plump in fawn jodhpurs, and fragrant with an irresistible combination of cupcakes and apricot soap—was the reason for Phin's extra-special grooming. Her mother had rung up the Chadwick that morning to say that Isabella would be coming to ride after school and to please make sure to have Dauphin ("doe-*fanh*") ready. Jack had almost asked, "Who?" before catching himself. It had been some time since Isabella had been to see her pony.

Dauphin is the French word for "prince." Phin thought it sounded very nice when being called out in a firm, ringing tone by a judge announcing the winner of a blue ribbon ("Miss Isabella Ingram on Dau*phin*!"), but privately he preferred Phin. Perhaps it was the fault of his father, whose outraged neighs Phin could still hear echoing down the bridle paths of memory:

*Just cuz du ain't got a face like a torn smuck like dy faider, du greetie-gowlie ting, don't mean du should be a haandless rool!**

Having a French name would somehow contribute to his uselessness in his father's eye, Phin was sure.

Poppy, a one-eyed, piebald terror who lorded over Phin and any horse or pony more than forty-six inches tall, had spent most of his career with a traveling carnival, giving rides to children. His association with carnies (carnival workers), rough-and-tumble life on the road, and frequent usage of the ancient Shetlandic dialect inherited from *his* father made him both hard to understand and hard to handle . . . at least for his son, whose good looks did little to earn Poppy's respect.

Phin had been born into the carnival life, but he'd always sensed he was destined for greater things. He found it dreary work, the endless slog around and around in circles, the long hours in the trailer as the carnival crisscrossed the country from county fair to state fair, Nevada's Cantaloupe Festival to Indiana's Pierogi Festival, Louisiana's Alligator Festival to South Dakota's Buffalo Chip Festival.

---

* Just because you're not ugly like your father, you crybaby, doesn't mean you should be a useless young pony!

Of course all the little girls wanted to ride him. . . . Oh, how they used to line up! They'd wait an extra hour just for the privilege of riding Phin instead of one of the other mousy, workaday ponies. This drove Poppy crazy.

Fat ones, thin ones, daft ones, screamin' ones—I'll bear 'em all and glad for the work! Mr. Precious-the-Boany-Rory only takes the little misses, eh? Ain't we particular, ye feckless peerie boy?

Oddly enough, Poppy *was* the second-most popular mount. Perhaps it was his piebald coat, the exoticism of his missing eye, or the palpable fire that flickered in the one that remained. The kids loved him, particularly the boys. The carnival barker liked to play them off each other, even pretending they were different breeds altogether instead of father and son.

"Who'd like to ride the prettiest pony in North America, South America, *and* the entire Shetland isles? The pony with the golden coat, the dainty step, and a disposition as sweet as pudding! He's a new penny, he is, and any lass who sits on his back will feel like a right princess. You, miss? Well, you're a lucky little girl, aren't you? That will be two of your ride tickets. . . .

"And now take a look at this fierce little man—all spirit, he is. He may have lost an eye, but he won the fight he lost it in! The perfect mount for a bold young boy like yourself. A pony with pride and dash! Yes, two tickets, please."

Any other children who'd gathered around during the barker's patter were hoisted onto the three other ponies who made up the string before they had time to be disappointed that they hadn't scored a ride on one of the two main attractions. They'd do a turn on Flossie, Barney, or Ignatius, and then as soon as their sneakers touched earth again, they'd be running to line up to fork over two more tickets for a spin on the golden pony . . . the prettiest pony in North *and* South America. . . .

Phin shook his head and snorted. He'd been rescued from all that. Rescued, in fact, by the man who was now giving him a light massage with the currycomb. Born into carnival life, like Phin, Jack had had bigger dreams, too. He wanted to do more than take care of a bunch of fair ponies. . . . He wanted to go to the big city, and Phin was his ticket there. Jack had known that someone as handsome as Phin should do more than drag kids around in circles all day. The pony leaned into his old friend with a sigh of pleasure. Drinking in the sweet smell of fresh alfalfa, clean bedding, and polished leather, Phin knew he was where he belonged. He hadn't turned out like his father, and thank goodness for that.

"Well, aren't we in a fine mood, laddie?" Jack smiled at him. "Thinkin' that life suits us pretty well? Glad your mistress hasn't forgotten you?"

An icy spur pierced Phin's reverie. Jack's lighthearted words had touched on a feeling—an uncomfortable, nagging feeling that had grown over the past few months—that Isabella Ingram wasn't spending quite as much time with her pony as she used to. Or showing quite the same level of ecstatic devotion, mingled with tyrannical bossiness, to which Phin had grown accustomed. But surely she was busy with school, and the weather had been uncertain. . . . Phin brushed aside his dark thoughts, gave Jack a little nip to make himself feel better, and resumed his contemplation of the pink and purple petunias. It was a beautiful day, and his mistress was taking him to the park. She would bring him a sugar lump. She loved him. And that was all any pony needed. Wasn't it?

. . .

PHIN WAS BRUSHED, COMBED, SADDLED, AND standing next to the mounting block at exactly three o'clock. And at 3:15. And at 3:30. By 3:45, Jack had to start feeding the other horses, so he tied the pony's reins in a knot and tethered him to a post near the barn's entrance, where Phin, bored and anxious, stared out into the busy city street teeming with children in strollers, children holding balloons, children with their nannies . . . but no blond-curled figure, sleek and well-fed like him, appeared. Finally, at 4:23:

"*Dauphin!* Did you miss me? Why are you tied up? Where's Jack?" These phrases were squealed in his ear as a pair of rosy, chubby arms, cinched by puffed sleeves, encircled his sturdy golden neck. Phin let out a sigh of relief. She had not forgotten him. Isabella's enthusiastic squeezes nearly throttled him, but the pony submitted, knowing that his reward would soon be forthcoming from her pocket. But Isabella seemed preoccupied with calling for her trainer, Hilda, and fiddling with her boots— new, Phin observed, and glossy with polish. He decided a reminder was in order.

"Stop it, Dauphin!" Isabella snapped. "You greedy little pig!" And with one gloved hand, she whacked the velvet muzzle that was lipping her pocket for its usual sugar.

It didn't hurt. It was only a little whack. But the humiliation! Phin had never been whacked by his mistress's hand . . . her crop, yes, but never her hand . . . and the tone of her voice! The pony jerked his head back and stared at her in amazement, but Isabella wasn't paying attention; she was tugging at his bridle, practically dragging him to the mounting block. Phin stumbled along at her side, reeling. She had hugged him and then she had hit him. Plus—and this was as upsetting to Phin as the blow—he hadn't gotten his sugar. What did it mean?

Phin stood quietly while Isabella mounted, jabbering to Hilda about the upcoming summer shows, which soothed him. He let his mind wander back to their earlier triumphs in the ring ("Miss Isabella Ingram on Dau*phin*!"). They were an eye-catching pair with their matching blond manes and correct form, so like the adults on their tall horses, except in charming miniature. Soon he would be bringing home more silver cups and blue satin ribbons for his mistress to display in the glass case by his stall. . . . The trophies now housed there had gathered a bit of dust, Phin had noticed. He hoped Isabella would speak to Jack about it.

Phin was jerked back to the present by a booted heel digging into his side. He bounced forward, eager to feel the spring sunshine, though that sunshine was now beginning to slant toward evening. As usual, Mrs. Ingram chaperoned their three-block walk to the park. Phin clip-clopped smartly down the avenue, unfazed by the taxicabs and limousines that passed on his right; the noise of pedestrians; the clink of plates and chatter pouring from the sidewalk café where Mrs. Ingram paused to accept the bottle of sparkling water held aloft by an aproned waiter, who in turn accepted the bill that fluttered from her fingers. All of this was the same as it ever was. And, as ever, cries of appreciation trailed in their wake:

"What a *beautiful* pony!"

"Look at that pretty little girl on that *beautiful* pony!"

"Mommy, *I* want a pony!"

"Daddy, can I pet the pony?"

Isabella Ingram sat up smartly, heels down, lower legs firm behind the girth, hands lightly clasping the reins. Phin arched his neck, picked up his hooves, pricked his ears. Mrs. Ingram sipped her sparkling water and waved a languid hand at the oncoming traffic, halting the line of cars so the pretty little girl and her beautiful pony could cross the boulevard and enter the leafy shade of the park.

Yes, all this was the same. And yet, perhaps because of Isabella's lateness, or the whack, or the missing sugar, it seemed to Phin as if the warmth had been sucked from the sunshine. His girth pinched, and his mistress felt heavy in the saddle. Suddenly the bridle path looked gloomy instead of dappled, and the bit dug into the corners of his sensitive mouth as he tried to hurry forward, away from the fearful sensations that buzzed around him like horseflies. Strangely, his side still hurt where Isabella had kicked him. And when she did it again, Phin realized why: She was wearing spurs. *Really*, Phin thought, *I'm doing my best, as ever. No need for these artificial aids.* And he trotted forward briskly, determined to please Isabella, to prove—to himself, to her, to anyone watching—that they were still a matched pair.

Though he moved ahead willingly, if not cheerfully, there was still something amiss. Isabella *was* heavy. Heavier than she'd ever felt before. Phin found himself struggling to maintain his pace, and when she asked him to canter, he took a few extra trotting strides just to gather momentum. He felt the spur dig into his side again.

"Come *on*, Phin! Canter!"

As if he didn't know what she wanted!

Normally, Phin liked nothing more than a brisk canter through the park. He enjoyed the drumming of his hooves on the packed earth of the trail, the feel of the breeze through his mane. But now he found himself tiring even before he and Isabella reached the gazebo overlooking the Japanese pond that was the traditional halfway marker of their ride. She spurred him on, and he did his best to obey. He felt her weight like a sack of grain on his back, inert and cumbersome. By the time she pulled him up, Phin was winded and breathing heavily. Isabella didn't seem to notice; indeed, she seemed determined to put him through his paces today. After what felt like only a moment of walking, she asked him to trot, then to canter again. Phin gamely moved forward, but as they rounded a tight corner between a corridor of birch trees, the weight of the girl, the discomfort of his girth, and his increasing fatigue finally took their toll. Phin stumbled badly, and Isabella nearly went over his head.

She shrieked; he stopped.

"What is the *matter* with you, Dauphin? You have gotten so *lazy*!"

This is just too much, Phin thought. She smacked him with the crop, and he flattened his ears and didn't move. She smacked him again, and he turned neatly around to face the direction of the stables. He had simply had enough, and nothing the frustrated and furious girl on his back could do would make him canter again.

It was a miserable ride back to the barn. Phin felt that he had never been so glad to be home, to see Jack, to know that a clean stall, fresh water, and a bucket of oats and sweet feed awaited him. He felt unpleasantly lathered and couldn't wait to get his saddle off and get a good rubdown. This was the one task related to his care that Isabella usually performed. She loved having these final leisurely moments with her pony, stroking his coat, feeding him carrots, talking her sweet, girlish babble in his ear till her mother dragged her away. But somehow Phin knew that today Jack would be doing the rubdown. Sure enough, after Isabella had flung herself dramatically from his back, she shouted for the groom.

"He was *awful*," she whined to Hilda and her mother as Jack made his way toward them. "He wouldn't canter, he practically *fell* going around a turn, and then he wouldn't go anywhere except back to the barn! He's gotten *lazy* and *fat*."

"Well now, Miss Izzy," came Jack's gentle voice, "he hasn't had much exercise lately, has he? You haven't been to see him in a while, and you don't let the other kiddies ride him. He can't stay fit without ridin', can he?"

"So this is my daughter's fault, is it?" snapped Mrs. Ingram.

"Well, not her fault that she's, ah, gettin' a bit big for him, no. I suspect she's a wee heavy for the lad now."

"*What?* Are you saying *I'm* fat?"

Jack's protests were drowned in a chorus of indignation from the mother and daughter. Phin sighed. All he wanted was his stall. All he wanted was the end of what had been a very bad day in the life of the most beautiful pony in the city.

CHAPTER 2

THE NEXT MORNING, PHIN DECIDED TO HAVE a talk with Van der Luyden. He was as eager to complain about his owner as Isabella had been to complain about her pony.

"Your owners don't visit you very much, do they, Van der Luyden?" he asked in a careless tone, between mouthfuls of alfalfa.

"Alas, no," Van der Luyden murmured. "My master passed away two years ago, and my mistress soon followed him."

Phin choked on his hay. How awkward.

"Erm, I hadn't realized. I'm, um, very sorry for your loss." Van der Luyden solemnly bent his head in acknowledgment.

"But, you know, when they were alive," Phin persisted, "did they ever, well, lose interest in you?"

"Certainly there were times when the affairs of the world, and I daresay affairs of state, prevented them from having the leisure to ride, yes."

It's not affairs of state keeping Isabella away, Phin snorted to himself. *More like affairs of playdates . . .*

But even as the sour thought went through his mind, he felt a sting of guilt. Isabella was his little girl. (Well, perhaps not his *little* girl.) She was his mistress. It was practically programmed into the fiber of Phin's being that he obey her in return for love and spoiling. And yesterday, he had not. The pony was overwhelmed by a sudden urge to confess.

"I disobeyed Isabella," he said abruptly.

Van der Luyden's only response was a subtle cock of his heavy head.

"I wouldn't canter. I mean, I *did* canter, but then I got tired." Phin's tone became more and more self-justifying. "My girth was pinching, and she used *spurs* on me—she's never done that before—and she wanted to go faster and faster and I just, I just . . . wanted to go back to the barn," he finished in a shamed whisper.

"I see," said the Friesian.

Phin took another small mouthful of alfalfa. "She said I was *fat* and *lazy*. But I'd tried my best, as I always do." An edge of indignation returned to his words. "She kept me waiting for over an *hour*. She hasn't been to see me in *weeks*. She didn't give me any sugar. . . ." Phin stopped himself, near tears. He risked a quick glance up at his companion. It was disconcerting how his view of Van der Luyden was always up his nostrils. However, the seventeen-hand stallion considerately lowered his head before answering the pony.

"Our bond with humans is ancient, and like all long relationships, occasionally fraught. While we may expect a certain amount of care and rational demands from our masters, it behooves us to recall that, ultimately, we may neither predict nor predicate their actions. I might suggest that it is our duty—our honorable and enriching duty—to attempt to meet these demands in as accurate and timely a manner as is within our personal capacity."

Oh, that's *helpful,* Phin thought. *See what I get for looking for some sympathy from the aristocracy . . .*

"I guess my 'personal capacity' was a little low yesterday," he grumbled. The stallion didn't answer. Phin knew Van der Luyden would sooner eat his water bucket than openly criticize anyone—particularly humans, but even ponies. He reserved his expressions of disapproval to a sort of chilly, thick silence; a subtle turning away of his royal Roman nose; and feigning sleep. Phin was getting the chilly, thick silence now. He decided to press the point.

"So I failed in my duty? Even though she doesn't come to see me? Even though it's her fault if I'm, if I'm, well, a bit out of shape? Even if she's . . . not very nice to me?" The Shetland's voice rose higher and higher, sounding childish even to his own ears.

The Friesian bent his head lower, causing his long, rippling black mane to swing forward. He fixed the pony's gaze with his, and his expression was serious but kind.

"We endure," he intoned, "even without sugar."

. . .

A WEEK PASSED, A DULL, ISABELLA-LESS WEEK. The weather grew even balmier, spring frothed even more frothily, and as the barn filled with children, Phin knew that school must be out for the summer holiday. And then on Wednesday morning, Jack appeared outside his stall, holding Phin's plush saddle over his arm and carrying his bridle in the other hand. The pony's ears pricked forward. On Wednesdays, he usually took his constitutional in the park . . . but apparently not today. *Isabella!* Phin gloated. *She* does *still love me. I knew she couldn't stay away once school was out! That must have been it—indeed, I was a ridiculous Shetland for worrying so.* (Or, as Poppy would have phrased it: *Ain't you da pernyim one? Ya skirl at a flee.**)

---

* Aren't you the fussy one? You scream at a fly.

He cast a cocky glance up at Van der Luyden, but the Friesian had fallen asleep after his morning oats and was snoring lightly in the comfortable gloom of the depths of his box stall. Looking at the gentleman giant, Phin vowed to be a perfect pony for Isabella today. Not that he would then brag to Van der Luyden—certainly not. He would simply allow word to spread—quietly, nothing pushy—of their renewed brilliance. Perhaps one of the grooms, while cleaning Van der Luyden's stall, would say to another, *Did you see how well our Phinny looked today? Miss Isabella said they had a very nice ride.*

Very nice? the other groom would protest, half laughing. *No . . . he gave her a* perfect *ride. What do you think, Jack?*

I think he's a perfect pony is what I think, Jack would say fondly, laying an affectionate hand on Phin's silken blond mane. Phin would bow his head modestly, perhaps just catching a glimpse of the old Friesian, his face shining with admiration. . . .

"Phinny, what are you up to? Get your head back up here so I can get this bridle on." Jack's impatient voice cut through his reverie. Phin snorted, realizing with embarrassment that in the midst of his daydream he actually had lowered his head in a coy fashion. He jerked it up hastily, bonking Jack on the nose. As his groom scolded him with language quite unfit for the Chadwick, Phin was heartily grateful that Van der Luyden was asleep.

. . .

BUT THE FIGURE STANDING BY THE MOUNTING block as Phin and Jack made their way down the last ramp was not Isabella. It was too slight to be his mistress, and on closer inspection, turned out to be a small boy, black-haired and imp-faced. Phin sighed. *Late again.* He'd been hoping that he and his owner could start the ride on a good hoof, but he felt the familiar resentment stealing over him. . . . How long would she keep him waiting today?

Phin couldn't have been more surprised when Jack led him straight to the mounting block, saying to the little boy, "Well, here he is, and what do you think?"

"He's fat," said the boy.

Jack grunted. "Nothin' that regular exercise won't cure."

"He looks like a *girl.*" The boy giggled, flicking Phin's silken forelock with one finger.

Jack hid what sounded suspiciously like a chuckle under a cough.

"Well, up you go," he said cheerily, and the boy sprang on Phin's back like a monkey.

Phin gazed up at Jack with an agonized expression.

Am I really going to be subjected to this? he pled with his eyes. Jack ignored him.

"So you've been on a horse before, right? This isn't your first time riding?"

The boy shook his head maniacally. "My parents took me to a dude ranch last summer, and that's when I decided I was going to be a cowboy! Giddyap! Hyah! Get along, doggies!" the boy shrieked as he began flapping Phin's reins up and down his neck. Phin stood stock-still, revolted.

"It's not quite the same—" Jack began, but he never got the chance to finish his sentence. With a piercing whoop, the boy took the reins in one hand and brought them down with an impressive amount of force on Phin's hindquarters. Instinctively, Phin bolted.

"No!" Jack shouted and began running after the fleeing pony. "Hold on there, Elliot, I'll catch him!"

But the boy wasn't frightened. He was thrilled.

"Hyah, Silver, hyah!" he screeched, pounding his legs into Phin's sides and waving the reins wildly. Phin lost his head completely and ran straight out the barn door and onto the street.

It was a nightmare version of his usual route with Isabella. Phin ran in a blind panic, sideswiping a taxi, nearly knocking over a stroller filled with triplets, and causing a waiter to drop his tray of iced coffees right onto the laps of three lunching ladies. Instead of cries of appreciation, shouts of anger and fear followed in their wake. Still the tiny cowboy on his back goaded Phin on, shouting his peculiar form of encouragement:

"Yee-haw! Hi-ho, Silver! *Yeeeeee-haaaaaaaaaaw!*"

It wasn't hard for Jack and Hilda to track the runaways. They simply followed the path of destruction–swearing cabdriver, screaming triplets, outraged ladies–to the park, where Phin, panicked into a state of total lunacy, had jumped into the fountain, sending Elliot over his head with a resounding splash. This is where the groom and trainer found them–Phin standing wet and wild-eyed beside a bronze mermaid, and the boy pounding the water with his fists, crowing.

"That was the best ride *ever*! Did you *see* us? I think I'll call her Goldilocks–Goldie for short! Hyah, Goldie, hyah!"

Phin shuddered, brought back to full, miserable consciousness by the boy's last words. *Goldilocks?* He turned pained eyes to Jack, and the groom was staring at him with a curious mixture of anger, laughter, and pity.

It was the pity that stung most of all.

. . .

THE NEXT TWO WEEKS WERE EXTRAORDINARILY confusing.

Since he and Jack had been sprung from the carnival, Isabella had been Phin's only rider. She insisted on it: No one was to have the privilege of mounting her beautiful pony, sitting in her tiny, impeccably polished saddle, besides herself. Now that rule—all of the rules of Phin's comfortable life, it seemed—had gone out the window. On Friday, he was again groomed, tacked, and led to the mounting block, where a weedy, trembling girl with glasses was standing, her arms folded around herself as if to keep her heart from popping out. That ride at least hadn't taxed Phin's energy; the weed was petrified of him and remained frozen in the saddle, weeping quietly, as Phin wandered aimlessly around the small ring. On Monday, he was subjected to two riders: a five-year-old boy who wet his breeches, sending a flood of pee down Phin's sides, and a hard-bitten gymnast in long braids who attempted to vault onto the pony's back as if he were a crossbeam. By the end of the week, the Shetland had been wept on, peed on, vaulted on, sneezed on, yelled at, and generally assaulted by a fairly representative cross-section of the city's younger set, and still no Isabella . . . and no explanation.

At first Phin thought he was being punished. Then it dawned on him that perhaps these children had been enlisted to give him the "exercise" he "needed" (the Shetland remained unconvinced of his lack of fitness). Either way, it was insulting. Isabella, he felt, should be getting him in shape herself, especially since the Fairmont Country Club Pony Show was merely weeks away. (Phin gazed wistfully at the silver bowl, still gathering dust in his trophy case, that they had won last year . . . "Miss Isabella Ingram on Dau*phin*!") Or, if this was his punishment for their one unhappy ride, surely enough was enough?

Phin struggled to find an appropriate response to the new regimen of riders he was expected to carry. He was tempted to refuse their commands altogether. On the other hoof, if he was the picture of a diligent, well-behaved Shetland . . . quietly submitting to an undignified fate . . . Isabella might be overtaken with remorse and longing for her perfect pony. Except that she wasn't around to watch him *be* perfect. And so Phin settled for apathy, performing the bare minimum required of him and no more. It felt low-class . . . school-horse-ish, even . . . and Phin shuddered to think what Poppy would have thought of his behavior (*Ya por aamus* *craetir!*)*, or Van der Luyden for that matter. That the two stallions, as much alike as corn dogs and caviar, should be linked in his mind in any way seemed preposterous, but Phin was certain that they would agree to disapprove of him.

All in all, life at the Chadwick, penthouse suite or no, had definitely taken a downwardly mobile turn.

---

* You poor miserable creature!

CHAPTER 3

A WEEK BEFORE THE FAIRMONT COUNTRY Club Pony Show, Phin started getting nervous.

That morning, Jack had again groomed and tacked him, and as he led Phin down the three ramps to the ring, the pony sullenly girded his hindquarters for another strange (and no doubt allergic, cowardly, or crazy) rider. He was just coming off a welcome break—he'd had no "exercise" except for his walks with Jack all week—and so it was with a heavy heart that he approached the mounting block, where a ponytailed girl stood wiping her nose on her sleeve. *Another allergic one.* Phin sighed.

But being sneezed on was not the chief of his worries. It was Isabella's attitude toward the pony show that concerned him. Her continued absence from the Chadwick showed a more than healthy confidence, and Phin supposed he should be flattered, but never had he felt so out of training for a big event. Of course, he probably was meant to be getting his conditioning from the string of pinch hitters, but they were hardly Isabella-quality riders. Van der Luyden took an unexpectedly rosy view of the whole situation.

"When my master and mistress went to the country house," he'd commented over their morning oats, "they were often thoughtful enough to provide me with exercise riders. I am glad to see that the Ingrams . . . second cousins, you know, to my departed mistress . . . are in the same habit. I'm sure you're learning as much from your young charges as I was fortunate to learn from Otto and Rosemarie. They still stop by for a carrot and conversation when they're in the neighborhood." The Friesian's eyes twinkled with fond reminiscence.

"Um," Phin said. There really was no reply to half of Van der Luyden's conversation.

Now, as the sniffling girl put her feet in the stirrups and timidly asked him to walk, Phin's conscience pricked. *Exercise riders* . . . The idea of *learning* from this motley crew was laughable . . . and yet, Van der Luyden had had a similar experience and he, of course, had probably found it "enriching." Perhaps, Phin mused as he sauntered slowly toward the trail, he wasn't being broad-minded enough. And what if Isabella arrived, dressed and ready for the pony show, that familiar hawkish gleam in her eye as she homed in on another trophy . . . and Phin was still "fat" and "lazy," as she'd declared him weeks before? With sudden determination, Phin injected a bit of spring in his stride and tucked his chin down to go on the bit. The sniffler didn't deserve it, of course, but he had to think of the big picture. She was simply the lucky recipient of his conscientiousness and talent.

And when Jack called out, "That's my Phin! You're lookin' yourself today, lad!" the pony's spirits lifted. It had been weeks since anyone . . . Jack, Isabella, Van der Luyden, his riders . . . had praised him (excepting the mad cowpoke, who hardly counted), and he'd almost forgotten what it was like, this lovely warm feeling that put even more bounce in his step and made the burden on his back seem literally lighter. Phin walked, trotted, halted, and turned circles with quiet ease, responding handily to the sniffler's most inept signals. He was even pleased when at the end of the ride, as Jack lifted her off his back, the girl squeaked, "That was amazing! I wish I wasn't allergic."

"Can't you take any medicine for it?" Jack asked.

The sniffler sniffed and shook her head. "It doesn't matter—my mom's already said no . . . but I had to ride him just once. He's the prettiest pony I've ever seen."

Phin felt a glow of pride, of well-being, return at her

words. Jack, however, seemed disappointed, sighing heavily as he led Phin back to his stall.

"What're we going to do with you, Phin?" He placed a work-roughened palm on the Shetland's neck. "The first time you're in form, the kiddo is takin' a joyride. Ah well."

Phin didn't understand his meaning; he was too absorbed in a daydream about the upcoming pony show . . . "Miss Isabella Ingram on Dau*phin*!" . . . to pay much attention.

. . .

THE WEEK BEFORE THE SHOW PASSED SLOWLY but comfortably in the penthouse of the Chadwick. Jack installed fans so the bright aerie was kept nicely cool, and was very particular about keeping the water buckets fresh. Phin's good behavior had made him pleased with himself, and when he was pleased with himself he was quite jolly. Instead of whickering whinily when Jack came by with his oats, he went back to his old carnival trick of picking up his bucket with his mouth and bringing it over for his friend to fill. Jack seemed inordinately touched by this, and instead of hurrying away to finish the rest of his chores, he often stayed a while, lounging on a hay bale and singing vaudeville tunes, accompanying himself with the battered harmonica he'd won in a dice game.

Lena, the queen of the uptown arena,
is the girl that I adore. . . .

Phin chased his last oats down, licking the bucket with satisfaction, and half closed his eyes. He loved it when Jack sang.

I love her half nelson, there's nobody else in the world who's so divine. . . .

The sky above the city faded to lavender and an evening breeze touched the leaves of the petunias in their window boxes. Jack was still singing when the first streetlamps blinked on, and he was still singing when the chimney swifts began flying home. Van der Luyden (whose depth of disapproval for any vestige of Jack and Phin's carnival life was profound) feigned sleep. The bells of the Episcopal church chimed softly as the smell of after-dinner espresso wafted skyward from the café and the sleepy voices of children were exchanged for the murmured conversations of lovers, sauntering hand in hand in the eternal romance of the city in spring. And still Jack sang in his low, sweet brogue, until Phin, full of oats and an undefined, melancholic longing, fell asleep.

. . .

THE MORNING OF THE PONY SHOW DAWNED hot and hazy. Phin opened an eye just as the sun's orange yolk crested the single spire of St. Peter's. He might be out of training, but the pony knew how early show mornings started, and he liked to be alert and mentally prepared before Jack appeared with halter, lead shank, leg wraps, fly mask, and the other necessities for making the three-hour trip to the country club comfortable. Last year, the year of the silver bowl ("Miss Isabella Ingram on Dau*phin!*"), Hilda had had Jack rig a small speaker to pipe classical music to the trailer, and Phin had indeed found it soothing. He hoped for a similar selection this trip . . . perhaps Vivaldi. . . . That was Van der Luyden's favorite. . . .

Phin was still contemplating the journey ahead, doing a positive visualization exercise that he'd heard Hilda talk about (*I see myself cantering on the right lead . . . I see my neat turns and precise halts*) when he heard Van der Luyden's soft "Good morning, Phineas."

" 'Morning," Phin mumbled, eyes closed. He wanted Van der Luyden to see that he was engaged in mental preparation and not to be disturbed. The Friesian, nothing if not perceptive, politely lapsed back into silence, which he broke only when Phin took a deep cleansing breath and fully opened his eyes.

"How are you feeling this morning?" the black stallion asked kindly. Phin's heart warmed at the obvious concern in his friend's tone. Of course Van der Luyden would remember that today was the pony show. . . . The old gentleman was thoughtful, in that noblesse oblige sort of way.

"Honestly, I've been a little worried," Phin confessed.

Van der Luyden bowed his head and gave his tail a gentle swish. "Perfectly natural, dear boy, perfectly natural."

"I'm glad that Isabella has such faith in me, and I did try to, erm, learn from my exercise riders. But, you know, I just have the jitters."

Van der Luyden was silent for a moment. "Yes, I'm afraid I did not entirely understand the situation before. I . . . commend your attitude, Phineas."

The pony ducked his head with pleasure. Van der Luyden's approval was not given lightly. Phin tried to resist the temptation to draw out the moment, and failed.

"Well, you see, I took your advice to heart. About learning. And even if I'm not quite as conditioned as I might be, it won't . . ." Phin searched for proper, modest words that the stallion would appreciate. "I daresay that if we don't bring home another silver bowl, it won't be from lack of effort on my part." *What a mouthful.*

A look of consternation came over the Friesian's face. *Oh no, did that sound braggy?* Phin groaned inwardly. *Should I have left out the part about the bowl? Did it seem too . . . greedy?*

"Of course, I know winning isn't everything," Phin said hastily. "It's the . . . spirit that counts. The, um, effort and, you know, doing your best for your mistress, and, erm, not expecting sugar all the time. . . ." Phin trailed off uneasily as the look on Van der Luyden's face turned from perplexed to sorrowful. *I've put my hoof in it now,* the pony thought with some exasperation. *Didn't mean to break the old man's heart by saying the wrong thing. My goodness but he's sensitive!* Luckily at that moment Jack's tousled head appeared around the door, and Phin was able to turn his attention away from the stallion without causing any further embarrassment.

The pony didn't expect a grooming—that would be done at the grounds of the country club, in the Ingrams' usual rented stall, third closest to the arena. It was, therefore, nice of Jack to give him a once-over with the soft brush, just for fun. But Jack himself didn't seem much in a mood for fun—his face was almost as long as Van der Luyden's. *I suppose they think things are going to go badly. Some faith they have in Dauphin!* The pony tossed his head in a marked manner as Jack attempted to comb his tumbling forelock. *Won't it be fun to see their faces when Isabella puts the new bowl—or perhaps this year a cup?—in the trophy case?* Phin glanced at the case in question, and then quickly looked away. There was something depressing about the faded blue ribbons, bleached by the sun, and the bowl, which didn't gleam in the light but instead looked rather dirty. *Well, they'll give it a good cleaning after the show, no doubt. No use resting on past laurels, after all.*

As Jack slowly packed up his brushes, Phin grew impatient.

"We'll hit terrible traffic if we don't leave soon ... everyone going to the country for the weekend," he grumbled to Van der Luyden, who persisted in gazing at his neighbor in a gloomy fashion. Then Phin felt Jack's arm slip under his neck as he pushed his muzzle through the halter and reached around to fasten the buckle. The halter felt oddly light and it didn't have the rich smell of oiled leather of which all the pony's tack was redolent. But it was comfortable—probably a new sort of lightweight summer fabric, Phin guessed. His eyes misted a bit at the Ingrams' thoughtfulness. . . . There *would* be Vivaldi, now he was sure.

Jack clipped an old nylon lead shank to Phin's (old nylon) halter, collected his brushes, and slid open his stall door. Then, seeing that Van der Luyden had his head over *his* door, Jack stopped and allowed the friends to touch noses.

"We'll miss him, won't we, old sir?" Jack stroked the noble stallion's Roman nose.

"Good-bye, Phineas," Van der Luyden murmured. "And best of luck to you. If you've . . . taken my advice to heart, I'm gratified. If I may be so presumptuous, your father and grandfather would be gratified as well."

Poppy? Phin reeled a bit.

"A pony can find honor . . . in many situations, as your forefathers were well aware," Van der Luyden explained. "That island of Shetland breeds very valiant creatures."

"Well, um, thanks, Van der Luyden," Phin said bewilderedly.

"And remember, Phineas . . ." But the old stallion didn't finish. It was the first time Phin had ever seen him at a loss for words.

" 'We endure, even without sugar?' " Phin hazarded.

"Yes, son. I suppose that will have to do." Van der Luyden sighed and touched Phin's small, rosy muzzle with his own aristocratic nose and then retreated to the back of his stall.

Downstairs, the bustle of last-minute preparations for the pony show consumed the small riding ring. A line of trailers stood double-parked and waiting on the street like taxis at a stand. Isabella and her mother would be somewhere nearby, although it was possible that they'd driven ahead; Phin was always delivered to shows in one of the Chadwick's trailers (hunter green with a large *C* and *O* monogrammed in cream on the side). Phin could see the back of a trailer now, and his ears pricked in anticipation.

As Jack led him toward the stable's entrance, Phin looked around for Isabella. It wasn't unusual for the Ingrams to go straight from home to the country club, but Phin had hoped to see his mistress once before they were engulfed in the bright, noisome chaos of the show grounds. It had been such a long time . . . and a reassuring pat wouldn't have gone amiss. . . . He couldn't find her, but the pony was touched to see that a veritable parade of the Chadwick's staff had paused in their work and were moving toward him, forming a kind of receiving line by the door.

First a crowd of grooms flocked around him, tousling his forelock with mock ferociousness, stroking his neck, and even kissing his cheeks. Then Mr. and Mrs. Brandish, the owners of the Chadwick, patted his back and told him to be a good boy, and a few of the stable's other clients came forward to stroke his mane and to say good-bye. Phin was utterly overwhelmed by the send-off. Never had a pony gone off to the fields of competition with such support, such admiration. Isabella and Hilda might not be there, but Phin felt the warm arms of the grand Chadwick Ostlers embrace him, and he knew that with such friends, he couldn't help but be ready for anything.

And then he saw her. Isabella, round and rosy and fragrant Isabella, fawn-jodphured and pink-manicured Isabella, was standing by the Chadwick's trailer, her hand on the gleaming leather halter of a leggy, silver-dappled Connemara mare who, unlike the girl at her head, was looking curiously at Phin. *That's not like her,* Phin thought. *Holding another girl's pony . . . and who is that, anyway? Some new first-floor tenant, I suppose.* Approaching his mistress, Phin put a bit of spring in his stride and looked alert. It was the perfect end to a perfect morning to have her there for a quick cuddle and conversation before the trip ahead.

But to Phin's surprise, Jack led him straight past the Chadwick's trailer and straight past Isabella, turning left toward a dirty, off-white, two-horse trailer hitched to an idling pickup truck streaked with mud and bird poop. Jack stopped abruptly and then half turned to Phin and muttered something too low for the pony to hear. Phin looked at him curiously. Jack turned him back around, took a deep breath, and again pulled him back toward Isabella.

"Wouldn't you like to say good-bye to your old friend, Miss Ingram?" he called out, and his normally melodious voice sounded harsh and strained. *That's right,* Phin sighed with relief. *Jack's been in a mood all day, and he can't even remember which trailer I go to or that obviously I should say hello to Isabella!*

Isabella didn't appear to have heard him, though they were standing only a few yards down the sidewalk from her.

"Miss Ingram?" Jack called again. Isabella appeared to be deep in conversation with another of the stable's riders, a redheaded boy named Tate who was looking admiringly at the fine-boned mare who stood quietly by Isabella's side. Phin couldn't understand it. He gave a low whicker of inquiry.

Isabella's eyes flickered in his direction at the sound. Their gazes met briefly, and then she turned back to the silver pony, clucking as she asked her to step up into the trailer, which the mare did with a dainty hop. And then Phin's mistress was gone.

CHAPTER 4

PHIN HAD SEVERAL LONG HOURS IN THE
trailer, which smelled strongly of goats, to try to convince himself that nothing was wrong. It was an uphill battle.

I'll see her at the country club. That's why she didn't feel the need to say hello. (Then why did Jack call it "good-bye"?)

That was Tate's new pony—she was just being helpful. (When has helpfulness ever been one of Isabella's primary, or even secondary, traits?)

This is a spare Chadwick trailer. There was some sort of problem with overbooking. (Why does it smell of goats?)

On and on, his mind spun futilely as the miles ticked by and the breeze from the half-opened window blew in first the smell of traffic and then the smell of cut grass and hay. Phin racked his brain trying to remember if this felt like the route to the Fairmont Country Club, but he couldn't be sure. He was alone in the trailer—also not a promising sign if he was here in the first place because

the trailers were overbooked—but at least Jack was driving. True, Jack had never driven him to a show before—
his work at the stable claimed most of his time—but
knowing that he was only a few feet away in the cab of
the poopy pickup was comforting.

The route may or may not have been familiar, but
one thing was, and discomfitingly so: the trailer itself.
The livestock smell; the cramped, swaying interior; the
way the trailer clattered over each small bump in the tar-
mac; and, most especially, having Jack at the wheel . . .
the only thing missing was a grumpy, one-eyed Shetland
hellion, aka Poppy, in the neighboring stall. *This was once
my life,* Phin thought. *How depressing.*

There was a sharp jolt as the trailer hit a bump—and
then another, and another. The pickup seemed to be dragging its cargo over a road laid out along the lines of the
wooden roller coaster at Coney Island, and Phin staggered as he tried to keep his balance. He heard Jack shout
something out the window of the cab, but it was lost in the
series of metallic shrieks and groans that the trailer gasped
out like a wounded animal. Phin prayed it wouldn't self-
destruct before they arrived at the Fairmont. Fairmont
Country Club—he could picture the soft velveteen swell of
the fairway and the blindingly white fences that edged the

riding rings, and he smelled the leather, clover, and organic fly spray smell that was the essence of summer luxury. He gave a tentative sniff out the window . . . and got a nostril full of the pickup's exhaust and scorched grass.

The sun cut a diagonal across the line of pasture, telephone pole, pasture, telephone pole, and pasture that seemed to stretch without end. Phin had lost track of time. And still the trailer lurched on.

It's a new route to the club.

The pony show changed locations.

His rationalizations grew weaker with every mile, but when the pickup finally moaned to a stop and the trailer settled into silence, Phin's ears still tried to make out the sound of girlish laughter, the tinkling neighs of blooded ponies, and the firm, ringing tone of the announcer, who would . . . soon, oh, let it be soon! . . . call out, "Miss Isabella Ingram on Dau*phin*!"

Instead he heard the sound of crickets, interrupted by a long complaint from a cow. Then he made out the crunch of Jack's boots on gravel as he swung down from the cab of the truck. Another squeal of rusty metal, and Jack was back in the truck and they were moving forward again—he must have stopped to open a gate, Phin reasoned. The next stretch of road was the bumpiest yet, and the pony's teeth chattered in his head as the trailer jackhammered along. Finally, after ten minutes of feeling like an oat rattling around in an empty bucket, the truck and trailer collapsed to a halt and Jack killed the engine.

There was, if he was honest about it, almost no chance that this pockmarked road led to the Fairmont. But Phin clung to hope till the very end, conjuring an image of the immaculate grounds so vivid that when Jack swung open the trailer door and backed the Shetland slowly out, he thought he saw, for one blissful moment, the verdant, shady lawns of the country club stretch before him. Then he blinked, and they were gone.

. . .

"IS THIS THE CITY SLICKER? HAW! TURN HIM around, lemme get a look at him."

Jack placed a gentle hand on Phin's halter and guided him toward the rough voice. Phin blinked in the glare of the evening sun slanting down on the shadeless gravel lot onto which he'd been deposited, and when his eyes found the giant leering down at him, he flinched.

"That's all right now, Phinny," Jack murmured. "Easy does it, laddie."

It was most certainly *not* all right, as far as Phin was concerned. The hulking man who stood before him looked like the worst kind of carnie—he was missing a front tooth, both arms were blue with full-sleeve tattoos, and his ripped, dirty tank top exposed rippling muscles that looked quite adequate to tear a Shetland pony in half just before devouring him. Phin's eyes showed their whites as he stared up at the monstrous being who appeared to be . . . chuckling.

"Haw, haw! Ain't he cute? Hey there, sweet pea, ain't you a little dolly? Huh? Ain't you just the prettiest thing?" The giant reached out one hand the size of Isabella's thigh and gave Phin's head a vigorous rub. The pony relaxed a bit: The giant might be uncouth, but at least he had eyes in his head.

" 'Sweet pea,' eh?" Jack still looked depressed, but he managed a small smile.

"What's it to ya?" the giant snarled, rounding on Jack like a caged bear that had just been poked.

"Nothin', mister, absolutely nothin'," Jack said mildly. "I call him 'laddie' myself, or Phinny. His original name was Phineas, which his little girl changed to Dauphin—French, you know—but he's always been Phinny to me."

The giant, pride soothed, relaxed his shoulders and stuck out the ham attached to his wrist.

"I'm Frank."

"Jack." They shook and Jack winced. "So," he continued, wringing out his hand, "you take care of the animals?"

"Yah, I come by once a week, more in the winter, but in the summer they got plenty to graze on. Check on 'em, make sure the water troughs are full. I got a nephew who stops by, too, an' feeds the ones that don't eat grass. Wish I could come oftener, but I got another job . . . and I gotta stick around where my parole officer can check up on me." Frank gave another, grimmer "Haw."

Phin saw Jack swallow hard. *Parole officer?* He cast a pleading glance upward. Surely Jack wasn't going to leave him alone with an ex-con the size of Van der Luyden? Plenty of former felons had worked the carnival, but Phin and Jack had always given them a very wide berth.

Frank the felon broke the awkward pause that had followed his words.

"Why's this little fella here, anyway? Somethin' happen to his owner?"

Phin practically held his breath, ears strained to catch the answer.

"Yeah, something happened, all right," Jack's voice was bitter. "She got big."

"Haw!" Frank laughed. "Girls'll do that. So she dumped him here. Shame, shame."

Jack sighed. "Frankly, ah, Frank, she coulda ridden him another year if she'd lost some weight. She was growin' more out than up, if you see what I mean. Easier to blame it on Phinny, maybe wanted something new. . . . We tried to sell him," Jack continued, and now his tone was a shade defensive. "But poor Phinny was out of condition–"

"Yah, he's a fat little thing, too, ain't he?" Frank interrupted.

"–and he wasn't showin' off his abilities as well as he might. Isabella–his owner–found her new pony before we found Phinny a new owner, and she needed the stall, so he was evicted, pretty much. Someone at the Chadwick knew about this place, so here we are. . . ."

The rest of the conversation dissolved around the pony, whose ears were ringing with the dreadful words . . . *evicted . . . dumped here . . . fat little thing . . . tried to sell him.* Shame rippled over Phin like an icy wind; he shook where he stood. His very bones ached with misery. He was being "dumped" . . . dumped the devil knew where, with an ex-felon for his new caretaker, all because he hadn't *shown off his abilities.* He cringed as he remembered his sulky, balky attitude toward the children he'd thought of as his "exercise riders" . . . that was what Van der Luyden had meant when he'd said he hadn't understood the situation! Oh, the allergic girl wouldn't have been so bad! Or the mad cowboy! Even the boy who'd peed on him! Phin pressed his small head against Jack's side, begging forgiveness, understanding.

". . . I'm hittin' the road for the summer—doin' a tour with the carnival as a favor to a friend—but I'll be back in the fall and I'll come by to check on the laddie."

Then Jack's arms went around Phin's neck, and Jack's stubbly cheek was pressed against his golden one. Jack's voice whispered words of encouragement in Phin's dully dangling ears . . . and what could only be Jack's tears dampened his creamy forelock.

"You're a tough lad, Phinny," Jack whispered. "Tougher than you know. Livin' soft hasn't knocked the grit out of you. You'll be happy out here, in the sunshine and the grass, out o' that dirty city. Sure, the Chadwick was posh an' all, but you'll be able to be a real pony out here. And it's better than bein' a carnival pony, right, laddie? You'll be happy, won't you, Phinny?"

Would he? As Jack hastily thrust the lead rope and the bag of Phin's brushes at Frank and jumped in the cab of the truck, revving its engine and peeling out of the gravel driveway in a cloud of dust and swaying metal, happiness seemed like a land as far away as home.

CHAPTER 5

T HE SUN WAS SETTING AND THE SILENCE that settled over the farm seemed louder to Phin than any city noise.

He stumbled along behind Frank, who was leading him toward a broken-down warren of low sheds, hutches, and a crazily crisscrossed fence line punctuated by a large, rusted aluminum gate. On the other side of that gate was the weirdest assortment of animals Phin had ever laid eyes on. He planted his forelegs in the gravel, yanking the lead rope taut.

"Aw now, sweet pea, nothing to be afraid of. Here's your new buddies, all ready to say howdy! Haw!" Frank patted Phin's neck enthusiastically and practically dragged him forward. Phin was quite sure that if he refused to move, Frank would simply pick him up and carry him under one arm.

The strange figures lurked by the fence in the gathering gloom. Heads sprouted monstrous horns the size of coatracks; small, slippery creatures scurried and yowled beneath the brambly hedges that lined the area by the nearest shed. Bellows, grunts, squeals, rasping barks: A raucous cacophony rose from the mob, and Phin dragged his hooves, eyes rolling white, nostrils flared in panic. He needed a plan.

If Frank was going to stick him in there with the howling beasts, Phin would have to act fast. His eyes, accustomed to the light pollution of the nighttime city, were having difficulty adjusting to the pitch black overtaking the last traces of dusk, but he could make out what looked to be a low-ceilinged, stall-like construction some ways to the right of the metal gate. When Frank led him in, he'd make a fast break, before the animals had time to react . . . then he'd hide in the stall and wait until daylight. Phin's very hocks shook: He hadn't had to make a run for it since he was a yearling and Jack had (nearly) caught him with his nose in the oat bin. And now he was fat . . . juicy . . . tempting . . . *No!* Frank wouldn't put him in with a horde of predators, would he? *Would* he? He was a felon! Maybe his crime was feeding ponies to lions! Or maybe that wasn't even a crime here! Oh, Jack! Oh, *Jack!*

Frank hummed nonchalantly as he unwound the

thick chain that fixed the gate to the unpainted wooden fence post. Phin tensed his small body, preparing for flight. Then the gate swung forward with a raspy sigh, Frank unclipped the lead shank from his halter, and Phin was alone with the menagerie.

He bolted before Frank's last pat could graze his hindquarters, bolted with every bit of speed he could muster from his short legs. He felt something smelly and hairy brush against his left flank, and then his right front hoof landed on something sickeningly squishy . . . and it squealed. Horrified, Phin squealed in return and plunged forward into the dark. There! He could just make out the shed and he ran headlong toward it, rounding the corner handily and leaping inside toward the darkest, most protected corner of the extraordinarily pungent stall. And then all hell broke loose.

The first feathery, clawed bomb went off between Phin's forelegs and he reared, smacking his head against the low ceiling. When he came down, three more squawking, flapping feather-grenades exploded by his back hooves, and then the very air around his head was filled with stinking feathers, wild cackles, and painfully sharp talons that scraped his sensitive muzzle and raked his soft golden coat. Blinded by the eye-watering stench and deafened by the shrieks of the crazed chickens, Phin bolted for the door, willing to brave the mob outside to get the heck out of the chicken coop.

As he ran through the deep, dark night, Phin could sense other animals somewhere near, at bay, watching but not approaching. He dug down for his instincts, dulled by his cosseted, stall-bound life, and he came up nearly empty. But he knew enough to run, to hide, and to wait until first light, when his poor eyesight would not put him at such a disadvantage. He plunged into a thicket of trees, pushing hard until he reached a small clearing where all was quiet and still. He stopped—flanks heaving, scratched nose bleeding, heart pounding—and waited for dawn.

. . .

WHEN PHIN WOKE UP, HE WAS SURROUNDED.

His first bleary, confused thought was: *Where am I?* The second was: *Oh no, I fell asleep!* And the third, once his exhaustion- and sorrow-addled mind registered the circle of animals facing him, was simply: *Oh no.*

It was early morning and the first light touched the leaves of the unkempt grove, overgrown with nettles, weeds, and choking vines that clung to the slender trunks of pin oaks. Phin stared wildly about him; it was as if he'd stumbled into the darkest heart of the city park, ungroomed, uncared for, lost to civilization. The only sounds were birdsong, the intermittent belching of frogs . . . and the stirrings of the motley triumvirate of beasts ranged before him. An enormous, dung-colored, humped creature stared down at him from heavily lashed eyes while his drooping lips chomped methodically, as if he were looking forward to tucking in to a nice breakfast of fresh pony. A rough-hewn, three-legged dog scratched himself casually, head cocked and tongue lolling from between his sharp white teeth. The last animal was the most frightening-looking of all: a mangy spotted rabbit staring up at him with red eyes charged with malice. Phin stared back, transfixed.

"That's Flopsy." The scruffy dog yawned. "You stepped on one of his cuzzins."

"Oh," Phin said. He'd never seen a meaner-looking creature than this bunny. He took a small step back and his rump pressed uncomfortably against a thorny bush.

"He wants you to apologize," continued the dog. "I reckon that—" But he was cut off by a sudden braying eruption from the giant, humped thing on the dog's right.

"Buht he's just uh little baby! He didn't know no better! Look at the little ba-a-a-by!" it bawled, forcing Phin farther back against the brambles. He turned bewilderedly toward the long-lashed creature blinking down at him with a now unmistakably benevolent expression.

"Cuh-ootchie cootchie coo!" Spit came flying from the long, forked upper lip as it bent its head down over the pony. Phin froze, unable to back away any farther, and felt the reeking strands of saliva hit his muzzle. He shuddered.

And then Flopsy took one menacing hop forward.

"I'm sorry!" Phin shouted. "I'm really sorry I stepped on your, erm, cousin! I didn't mean to, I swear! Please don't . . . don't . . ." Phin wasn't sure what exactly he feared the rabbit would do, but he felt sure he was capable of horrible things. Childishly, he squeezed his eyes shut, as if the animals would disappear if he couldn't see them. Many seconds of silence ticked by, and then he heard the dog's raspy growl:

"You can open your eyes if you want. He's gone."

Phin raised his lids a millimeter and breathed a sigh of relief. Flopsy had indeed left the clearing.

"Probably a good idea, apologizing," the dog commented. "That's one mean bunny. You don't want to get on the wrong side of him, or any of the Fuzzy Butts, for that matter."

"The *what?*" Phin squealed.

"Fuzzy Butts. It's a family name. There's a whole slew of 'em aroundabout here. You want to stay out of their way. I ate one of Flopsy's stepnieces a few years back, and well . . ." The dog looked meaningfully at the space where his left front leg should have been. Phin gasped in horror.

"The Fuzzy Butts took off your leg?" he whispered.

The dog gazed at him solemnly for a beat, then burst into tongue-wagging laughter, chasing his tail in delight.

"No, you goof! They're *bunnies*! I'm part Catahoula, part shepherd, part pit bull, and not an ounce poodle! You think a bunch of rabbits could take me?"

Phin remembered the red gleam of hate in the bunny's eyes. "Yes," he said frankly.

"Ha!" the dog barked. "You, maybe. Not me. Not Freddy. It took a Mack truck to part me with my old leg, and that's a fact. That truck was the only thing that's ever beat me in a fight, and it wasn't a fair fight neither," he added, scratching an ear with cocky nonchalance.

Phin was thoroughly confused, but wanted to keep up. "Why wasn't it a fair fight?" he inquired.

"Huh. 'Cause it had five hundred and sixty-five horses under its hood and eighteen wheels under its belly, and I'm, let's see, a *dog*?" He snorted. "Not exactly on the stick, are you, Goldilocks?"

"Don't call me that," Phin cried, stung.

"Well, what should I call you? You didn't exactly let Frankie introduce us properly last night. In fact, you stomped Flopsy's cuz, then took off for the chicken coop and stomped a few birds. That ain't what my old master would call 'an auspicious beginning,'" Freddy growled.

The dog's description of the previous night was too accurate to deny, and Phin felt the little puff of pride deflate. He hung his head, at a loss for words.

"Pore luhttle baby," the humped animal murmured sadly. "Just a luhttle guy."

Phin managed an upward glance, slitting his eyes in case any more toxic spit came flying his way. "I'm sorry, but what exactly *are* you?" He addressed the question to the creature's cavernous nostrils, which hovered over his head, fouling the air with a moist fug.

"May-aybe I cuhn be your daddy?" the beast bleated hopefully. Phin just stared at him.

"This wet rag? This is a camel. You know, people ride 'em around in the desert, can go weeks without water, blah, blah, blah. This one goes by Wally. Mostly he's dumb as a rock," Freddy explained.

"I'm not a baby, Wally," Phin said firmly. "I'm a Shetland pony. We're a very popular breed."

"Sure, I bet you got lots uh luhttle buddies." Wally the camel sighed fondly.

Freddy rolled his eyes. "Well, time for this dog to make dust. See ya 'round, Blondie." With a grace and speed Phin would hardly have thought possible, given Freddy's conspicuously absent limb, the part-Catahoula, part-shepherd, part–pit bull made a hopping turn and proceeded to bounce jauntily from the grove, his long, feathered tail swinging rhythmic circles behind him, as if it were the dog's propeller.

"Wait!" Phin cried. "Don't leave me!" As soon as the words were out, Phin heard how pathetic he sounded, but he couldn't care, not when this great, aching hole was taking over his heart once again. The hole where Jack and Isabella and Van der Luyden and the Chadwick . . . his whole life . . . had been.

Freddy paused mid-hop and glanced over one powerful, sloped shoulder. His quizzical expression softened a fraction toward pity.

"Well, come on and agitate some gravel. Guess I can hang 'round this burg for a spell, maybe show you the ropes. . . ."

Phin trotted forward gratefully. "My name's Phin," he said. "My full name is Dauphin . . . it's French for 'prince,' but most everybody calls me Phin or Phinny."

"Sure, Prince Blondie." The dog laughed at him. "Prince Phinny from the city!" He gave a great bark of amusement and bounded ahead, Phin jogging resignedly behind him.

"Wait fuh me, Prince Ba-a-by!" Wally wailed, and the threesome made their noisy way through the forest.

CHAPTER 6

IN THE BRIGHT SUMMER-MORNING LIGHT, PHIN was able to take better stock of his surroundings. It didn't take long for him and Freddy and Wally to clear the last of the woods—in reality, not quite the primitive jungle Phin had thought, but more of a forgotten waste of bramble, bush, and skinny, nondescript trees spreading out from a river that Freddy told him was about half a mile away.

"Can't get to the river from the farm, but we got a crick that runs off it. That's where Miss Sumalee hangs out."

"A *what* hangs out *where?*" Phin asked.

"Not a what—a who. Sumalee. Great gal. Water buffalo. Likes, oh, let's see, *water?* So she hangs by the crick." Freddy affected an exasperated tone, but Phin suspected he enjoyed the pony's ignorance. Phin still didn't know what the "crick" was, but he didn't feel like giving Freddy the satisfaction. As he trotted along beside him, Phin cast a sideways glance at his uncouth companion. Freddy was medium-size, he supposed—smaller than the Weimaraner Phin was acquainted with from the park, but considerably larger than Mrs. Ingram's Yorkshire terrier. His ears flopped to the side of his broad forehead, and the left ear was shorter than its partner. Phin noted the ragged tear where the tip of the ear should have been and guessed it had been lost in a fight. The dog's short coat, though rough with dust, was a showy collage of black, white, and gray patches more splotches than spots; his paws and chest were white, as was the tip of his incongruously elegant, feathered tail. He was wiry but strong, without an ounce of flesh to spare. Suddenly, Freddy turned and grinned at Phin, and the pony saw that he was also missing a front tooth: the final rakish touch to one tough mutt.

Phin looked away, but not quickly enough. "Take a picture, it'll last longer, Prince Blondie," Freddy barked. Phin tossed his forelock and stared with a sudden (feigned) interest at the surrounding countryside.

There wasn't much to see. A flat field, speckled with burdock and onion grass, stretched north from the woods that hid the river. Bordering the field was a ragged, weather-beaten fence line, so warped and missing such a variety of boards that Phin couldn't imagine it had much power to keep anything in—or out. At the opposite end of

so. He just did the water yesterday, before you showed your pretty little face. Delivered a coupla kids. Got the reindeer loose from the fence. The usual." Freddy yawned. "Ziggy–that's Frank's nephew–he'll be by tomorrow to drop kibble for the cats, stuff like that. If he remembers. He's scared of anything bigger than a bread box, though, so don't expect much conversation from *him*."

Phin digested this in silence. An entire week, or more, without human company. He was afraid of Frank, but not as much as he was afraid of being alone. He tried to sound casual when he asked, "And the kids? Where did Frank deliver them?"

"Um, in the barn? In the field? How the heck would I know? I can't keep up with 'em." Freddy looked mildly disgusted.

"So there are *lots* of kids around here? Frank brings them regularly?" Phin's spirits slid upward a notch–perhaps there might be some little girl, or boy, who would be glad to find a beautiful pony in this desolate waste.

"Sure, the place is lousy with 'em. But mostly their mamas bring 'em. Frank just helps out if the nannies are havin' trouble."

Phin gave a little shudder. He could imagine what Frank did with the naughty children. He briefly wondered if Frank could take on Isabella before deciding that even the tattooed giant would be overmatched by his mistress. Still—kids! Lots of them! Phin peered ahead hopefully toward the driveway and barn.

"If you're so gone on goats, you'll have a blast here," Freddy growled. "Me, I like to talk, and goats don't talk— they just eat and make more goats. But don't let me rain on your parade."

"Who said I liked *goats*?" Phin snorted, glad for once to be the one doing the correcting. "I'm simply looking forward to meeting some of the children—whom I'm sure will be more than happy to see *me*—but I have absolutely no interest in goats, thank you very much." He lifted his muzzle just a touch.

Freddy's howl of laughter was long and unnerving. Phin tried to look unconcerned, even contemplated slowing down to wait for Wally, who was wandering dreamily in their wake, mumbling to himself and occasionally attempting to plant a sloppy kiss on Phin's hindquarters. But Freddy wasn't about to let him off so easily.

"Not *that* kinda kid, you dumb blond!" the dog yapped delightedly. "I was talking about baby goats! You think any ankle-biter hangs out here? Maybe once upon a time, back before the highway got built, but no one drives by the Funny Farm now, unless they're lost. Sorry, Prince Pony—it's just us folks and Frank. Ain't we good enough for you?" Freddy leered at him.

Something was tugging on Phin's tail. He turned and saw that Wally had taken a big mouthful of the soft golden strands and was chewing contentedly. "Yummy ha-a-ay," he sighed.

No, Phin thought as he tried to remove his sodden tail from the mouth of the camel. *No, you're not good enough for me.*

· · ·

MEETING THE REST OF THE FUNNY FARM'S IN-habitants did little to change that opinion. The place was, as Freddy said, lousy with goats, all of whom seemed to be enormously pregnant or nursing baby goats. Oddly, Phin had yet to see a billy goat, and he mentioned this to Freddy.

"That's our little local mystery," Freddy said in a carrying whisper. "No one's ever seen a daddy goat . . . just nannies and kids. Must be something in the water."

In addition to the tribe of goats, Phin was introduced to, or saw at a distance, the rest of the farm's boarders. There was a bizarre-looking, leggy, feathered creature called Matilda. The thing with the coatrack antlers turned out to be a mild-mannered, blind reindeer named Sven—the same reindeer who frequently got his antlers stuck between the slats of the fence while he was grazing. Sumalee the water buffalo could not be coaxed from the "crick" (or creek, as Phin now understood it to be), but she sent a vague bellow over the field that Freddy assured the pony was a warm greeting.

"She's a real doll face, that heifer," Freddy said fondly. "Usually you ungulates are dumber than turds, but she's got brains between those big ol' horns. More'n you can say about the guy who put her here. Thought he'd start a craze for water buffalo milk—'WaBuMi' he was gonna call it. I'm gone on Sumalee, but no way in heck I'm gonna drink her WaBuMi, if you catch my drift. And I'll drink a lot more things than a durn person will—except maybe my old master, Charlie. He'd drink paint. Probably *did* drink paint, come to think of it." Freddy turned his head and snapped at a flea.

"So he put Sumalee here . . . ?" Phin didn't want to complete his thought (*like I was put here*) so he let the sentence trail off.

"Righto. Haven't you caught on yet? This is Nowheresville. Everybody at the Funny Farm is here 'cause they got nowhere else to go. Who's gonna keep a water buffalo once they figure out they can't make any beans off her?"

"They closed down my zoo-oo-oo," Wally sighed lugubriously.

"I was almost made into a *purse,*" squawked Matilda. "They had me pegged as an ostrich, the ning-nongs."

"Instead of a . . . what, precisely?" Phin thought Matilda might be a bird (feathers, beak) or perhaps a giant lizard (scaly legs, nearly bald head).

"An *emu,* you galah! Got a few 'roos loose in the top paddock, don't you?" Matilda gave her feathers a light fluff while staring down her beak at the confused pony.

"The goats and bunnies get dropped off regular," Freddy continued. "Cats just show up. Sven got separated from his herd somewheres up north and still ain't sure how he ended up here. . . ."

"We migrate great distances," Sven commented, "so not being able to see put me somewhat at a disadvantage." His voice put another knife of homesickness into Phin's belly. He had a touch of Van der Luyden's courtliness and a lilting accent that reminded Phin of Jack. The pony heaved another sigh.

"So how 'bout you, Prince Blondie? What's your sob story?" Freddy cocked a ragged ear and the other animals looked expectantly at Phin. Being the focus of so many strange sets of eyes, from Matilda's glistening black beads to Sven's softly clouded irises, in so many strange faces, made him feel uncharacteristically shy. Phin ducked his head, shifting his weight from one leg to another.

"Have *you* got his tongue, Maxie?" came a sudden yowl from the direction of the chicken coop.

"Not *me*—how about you, Mixie?"

"Nah, must be Moxie!"

"SHUT IT, YOU PUSS IN POOPS!" Freddy roared. "NOBODY THINKS YOU'RE FUNNY!"

"You would if you weren't too stupid to understand us, mutt!"

"No appreciation for self-referential wordplay!"

"Go bark up the wrong tree!"

"I'M ABOUT TO TAKE A COUPLE OF YOUR NINE LIVES!" As Freddy leaped to his three paws, hackles raised, the voices dissolved into a shrill caterwaul of jeers, razzes, and abusive language, then faded away.

"Cats?" Phin ventured.

"Of the worst variety," Sven said mournfully.

Though undoubtedly obnoxious, Phin couldn't help but feel grateful for the reprieve Mixie, Maxie, and Moxie's interruption gave him. Freddy hopped off in the direction of the chicken coop, growling insults, and Sven and Wally resumed grazing. Phin turned pointedly away from Matilda the mammoth lizard-bird and wandered back over the field he'd just crossed. He sniffed the yellowing crabgrass and took a listless nibble. It tasted like dust. He felt the sun beating down on his golden coat and knew he was going to get a burn. He was thirsty. But mostly, oh mostly, he was alone. *Nowheresville.* As Phin stood in the middle of the field, eerily silent in the midday heat, he realized fully for the first time that no one was coming back for him. *This* was his new home. He was now a member of the Funny Farm.

CHAPTER 7

*D*U AIN'T NO BETTER THAN A MARK, DU AIN'T, *du peerie pony. Du is dy midder's bairn, and no mistake. Not that I'm smackin' down dy midder, mind. I'll nae forget the day she came trottin' past the floss wagon.* * *Outside of Natichoches it was—she was enterin' some contest . . . pullin' a braaly*[†] *white cart all bedecked with posies. But dy midder was better'n any posy. Gold all over, like you are, with the sweetest expression on her boany*[‡] *face, but fire in her eye! Aye, she was an arg*[§] *one. She won that contest, then I won her—ha!*

Phin always shuddered to think what form Poppy's wooing of his mother had taken. Over time, his memories of the golden mare he so much resembled were gilded into myth. He'd had less than a year with B&B Barn's

---

* You're no better than a sucker, you little pony. You are your mother's child, and no mistake. Not that I'm insulting your mother, mind you. I'll never forget the day she came trotting past the cotton candy machine.

[†] Pretty

[‡] Beautiful

[§] Fiery

Summer Serenade (Serena for short): Her owner, disgusted that his champion American Show Pony had been put in the family way by such a low-class rogue, had dumped Phin at Jack's trailer when the carnival had come back to town the next season.

Standing alone in the parched field of Nowheresville, Phin closed his eyes and tried to conjure up his mother's limpid eyes, the feel of her velvet muzzle touching his flank as he nursed, the freshly shampooed smell of her penny-bright coat. And yet, the time he'd spent at her home hadn't been an altogether happy one. He was the hard evidence of Serena's fall from grace, and thus, at best, ignored by the B&B's owners and staff. Like so much in the pony's past, it was complicated.

No, Phin thought, *the only place I've been truly happy— the only place where I've been appreciated—was the Chadwick.*

Jack had taken him from the drudgery of carnival life, had brought him to the Fairmont Country Club Pony Show (where the halter class trophy was presented to them practically on bended knee), and had sold him on looks alone to Hilda Holzen, head trainer at the grand Chadwick Ostlers. The Chadwick proved to be a home for them both: Jack got a job as a groom, was quickly promoted to barn manager, and settled into city life as happily as his friend.

And yet, and yet... had he ever *really* belonged there? This was the question that was now tormenting Phin and dragging forth the echoes of his father's contemptuous harangues. The pony felt sore all over: stiff from the long, bumpy trailer ride; heart-sore from missing Jack and from being abandoned and unloved in general; and now his brain hurt from thinking, an exercise he generally avoided doing to any strenuous degree. He was also thirsty—and that at least he could do something about.

The "crick" wound haphazardly through the Funny Farm like a tangled, discarded ribbon. The first spot that Phin approached was a discouraging, muddy-brown trickle purling between steep banks that looked too difficult for the pony to navigate. But as he continued downstream, Phin discovered what a changeable creature the small stream was: It swelled unexpectedly to a torrent chattering over rough gray stones, flattened out to a tranquil pool flickering with fish, and generally traipsed along in a most inconsistent fashion. Phin was so occupied with following its progress, and puzzling over the best drinking spot, that he'd entirely forgotten that the creek was also the favored haunt of Sumalee, the water buffalo.

At first Phin thought that a large boulder had fallen into the stream. This was disappointing, as the bend was by far the nicest he'd yet found—wide and deep, with a clear path down the banks and a pleasantly shady canopy of trees overhead. And then the boulder addressed him.

"Good afternoon," it said.

Phin shied in surprise, taking a few skittering crab steps away before realizing that what he had taken for rock was, in fact, a very large animal. At least, Phin assumed she was large: The only parts of her above water were her head and the side of her boulderlike belly, brown with mud and slick with water. She looked a bit like a cow, Phin thought, but closer inspection belied the comparison. There was more intelligence in her dewy, heavily fringed eyes and more grace in the magnificent horns that swept back from her lined brow than Phin had ever seen in a cow. Even the shape of her prominent nose, rising up from the end of the long, firm swoop of her face, was distinctive. All in all, she wasn't very terrifying, despite the horns, and Phin sidled back to the bank.

"Oh, hello," he said in an offhand manner, "I didn't realize this part of the, er, crick was taken."

"Not taken—only borrowed. You're welcome to join me, if you wish." The water buffalo's voice was mellow and almost sweet.

"Pardon me, but I don't wallow," Phin said stiffly.

"Well then, come down for a drink. There's a nice spot just upstream from here. That trail goes right to it." The water buffalo blinked pleasantly at him, then eased to her side, submerging most of her head. She sighed contentedly and ripples of water danced away from her face.

Phin picked his way neatly down the muddy trail and placed a tentative hoof in the stream. The water felt deliciously cool. So deliciously cool, in fact, that it soon became quite tempting to wallow. Instead, well-bred Shetland that he was, Phin moved carefully upstream until he judged he was far enough away from the water buffalo to make their shared bathing and drinking place palatable.

It was a novel experience, not drinking from a bucket. It took a bit of getting used to, the way the water swirled around his nose and fetlocks and had an almost tangy, mineral taste. After several minutes, Phin raised his dripping muzzle and gave a small snort of satisfaction.

"Nothing better than Adam's ale, as Freddy calls it," the downstream water buffalo commented.

"You're Sumalee?" Phin turned gingerly around, testing the ground before each step.

"Yes, and you must be Phin, the city pony." The Shetland gave silent thanks that Freddy hadn't told her that his name was Prince Blondie or Goldilocks.

"The farm must be a little different from what you're used to," Sumalee continued, a gentle question in her voice. Phin gave a curt nod. It was suddenly difficult to keep misery and self-pity at bay, with Sumalee's kind gaze fastened so sympathetically on him.

"Tell me about it," she said simply.

And Phin did.

. . .

"I JUST CAN'T BELIEVE ISABELLA DIDN'T EVEN say *good-bye.*" Phin knew he was starting to repeat himself, but the luxury of having a good listener was too dear to relinquish quite yet. He was lying comfortably on the sandy floor midstream, his legs tucked neatly beneath his belly, in what he thought was a genteel approximation of a wallow. He had to admit it felt very nice.

"Usually humans are more sentimental than animals, but occasionally they're decidedly *not,*" Sumalee said. "It seems your Isabella was of the pragmatic variety, as was my owner."

Phin was pondering whether it would be rude to ask Sumalee about her WaBuMi, when she changed the subject.

"What about your family? What did your father and mother do?"

Phin hesitated. But there was something about the water buffalo's expression, a kind of calm interest that was neither idle curiosity nor urgent questioning, that reassured him.

"My mother was a champion show pony, in driving. She pulled a little cart and won all sorts of trophies. Poppy . . . well, Poppy worked for the carnival, giving rides to kids. That's, um, actually what I did, too, before Isabella . . ." Phin looked away in embarrassment.

"What an impressive variety of usefulness you ponies have," Sumalee said robustly, smacking at a fly with her whiplike tail. "No wonder you're such survivors."

"Come again?" Phin was pleased to be thought of as impressive, but he wasn't clear on the water buffalo's point.

"Well, at the risk of sounding prideful, let's take the example of my animals, the water buffalo. We have partnered with people since ancient times. We have plowed rice fields, pulled carts, provided milk. We have fought the tiger and the crocodile. We have run with the Crusaders. We are a farmer's wealth, and often his best friend. Well-rounded, wouldn't you say?"

And depressingly utilitarian, Phin thought. "But do you ever get to have any fun?" he blurted.

Sumalee's voice was melodious, her presence was calming—but she had a belly laugh like a stevedore. Phin pinned his ears back at the spluttering bellow that shot droplets of water over his face and mane.

"Lots of it, actually," the buffalo chuckled, sending another watery spray in Phin's direction. "Many villages and towns hold festivals in our honor. There are parades, races, very exciting fights, and even beauty pageants. In Thailand, where my ancestors are from, the children make costumes to look like us. There are feasts and music. . . . Ah, it's a wonderful time."

Phin felt a stab of envy, mingled with awe. *A festival in her honor . . . a beauty pageant . . .* The pony had a vision of himself with a wreath of roses around his neck, walking with quiet dignity at the head of a long procession, a Shetland-themed song belted out by a chorus dressed in golden robes, children tossing flowers in his path. . . .

"You see," the water buffalo interrupted this pleasant vision, "we are intimately connected with people, in all sorts of ways. It's very nice to be appreciated, but many times the work must be its own reward."

Phin had a thought. "'We endure, even without sugar,'" he said. "A friend of mine told me that."

"Your friend is wise," the water buffalo said. Phin felt very grown-up. It was that sort of conversation. But then he had another thought.

"But sometimes the work kills you," he said softly. "That's not much of a reward."

The lines around Sumalee's eyes deepened until they looked like plow furrows curving up to her brow.

"Ye-e-s, that's so," she said slowly. Then she stopped and looked at Phin, and under her kind regard he told a secret that no one knew—not even Jack.

"My gutcher—sorry, that's Shetland for grandfather— he was a pit pony. Do you know what that means?"

Sumalee shook her head.

"Well, he worked in the coal mines, pulling carts loaded with coal. We're so small, you see—we can fit in the mine shafts. I don't . . . I don't think he saw the light of day after he was three years old. He lived in the pit, breathing that foul air, not knowing night from day. And then, well, there was a cave-in, and he was trapped, along with several other ponies and miners. They never were able to reach the bodies. Poppy told me there's a marker, like a grave marker, above the mine . . . but it doesn't mention my gutcher or the other ponies. Just the miners."

"You must be very proud of him," Sumalee said quietly.

Phin was surprised—it was the first unintelligent thing she'd said. *Proud of my gutcher?* Phin thought bewilderedly. *What's there to be proud of? He was worked like a slave and died like a slave, forgotten and unmourned. And then crazy Poppy took him as a role model. . . . "I'll go out horizontal, just like Faidir!" he used to say . . . and he did. Dropped dead in his tracks. His final action was to make sure he didn't roll over on the child he was carrying as he took his last breath. Phin had never seen Jack cry before that terrible day.*

"Jack saved me," he said abruptly, not caring if he repeated himself or if he didn't make sense. "*My* work won't kill me. The work *I* do is for honor—to be recognized as the best. I'm the kind of pony that wins awards, like my mother. Jack saved me," he insisted in a high voice that sounded lonely to his own ears.

"There is honor in all work, Phin," Sumalee said gently. "Even the kind that doesn't get trophies."

Jeez, is Van der Luyden part water buffalo, or is Sumalee part Friesian? Phin wondered with exasperation.

"Sure, sure," he said, clambering to his feet and giving a modest shake that was more of a shimmy.

Sumalee cocked her head and a hint of amusement touched her eyes. "So here you are," she said.

Phin looked up at the dense canopy of green above, looked around at the nondescript green and brown that hemmed the creek, and looked out to the hot, dry field beyond the edge of trees.

"The Funny Farm is a gift, you know," Sumalee said.

Phin snorted with disbelief. "Some gift," he muttered.

"We are 'unwanted' animals—useless, redundant, or damaged . . ." Phin winced at the company with which he was being lumped.

". . . so what does that mean? It means we are free. In a man's world, an animal that is useless is free. Some are truly free in the wild, some are hunted as pests, and a few find the limited, but safe, freedom of a home like this. The question is what you do with your freedom."

"Freedom's just another word for nothing left to lose," Phin said crossly.

"Exactly," said the water buffalo in a satisfied voice. "Because, Phin, when you've lost everything, sometimes you find yourself."

CHAPTER 8

Phin was only about halfway across the field before the sun had baked him nearly dry and Sumalee's words had gone from sounding half-baked to scary. Scary, because Phin had been certain he knew himself, down to his hooves. The suggestion that he had lost more than a home, more than a former life—that somewhere along the way he'd lost *himself* and now needed to be found—was disconcerting to say the least.

But as he discovered, in the scorching, endless weeks that followed, the one thing he still had—and had in buckets—was time. Time to think, time to remember, time to sulk, and, most of all, time to be bored out of his skull. His life at the Chadwick had not been a particularly active one, to be sure, but its leisured pace was nicely structured around his comforts and care. He'd had the benefit of refined conversation with a horse from one of the city's oldest and best families (*not that I took advantage of it,* Phin thought with a twinge of guilt, *but Van der Luyden* *was so* stuffy!*). He'd had access to the smoothest, leafiest bridle paths (*and I just wanted to go back to the barn!*). He'd had his own set of brushes; his own leather tack; a view of one of the city's toniest blocks through a picture window rimmed with flowers. Even his water bucket had had his name on it, and Isabella would have been horrified if any other Chadwick horse had used it. And, of course, he'd had his very own trophy case.

Now he was living in what was for all intents and purposes a commune . . . or a prison, as he often thought, despite Sumalee's talk of freedom. If he was thirsty, and didn't want to walk all the way to the crick, he had to wait in line at the water trough, flecked with grass and hay and camel slobber and often undrinkably warm. One day in early August, Phin saw Sven go to town on the salt lick, and the pony realized that after you've seen a blind, melancholic reindeer attack a salt lick, you'll never be able to so much as nibble the thing again. It didn't help that after Sven was done, he got his antlers stuck in the fence, and Frank wasn't due for another three days. The reindeer didn't complain—that was almost the worst of it. All he did was sigh heavily and settle down with resignation written all over his knobby-kneed body. After an hour of listening to the just-audible exhalations, which had "Oh, don't worry about me, I'll just sit here with my antlers in the fence and rot, you all go on and have a nice time" written all over them, the reindeer had gotten on Phin's last nerve.

"Can't someone *do* something about Sven?" he asked Freddy crossly. "Surely he's not going to lie there and *sigh* like that for three days?"

"His record's seven." Freddy yawned.

"And you just *let* him?" Phin thought if he had to listen to the heavy breathing any longer, he might go stomp on a chicken just to relieve the tension.

"What do you expect *us* to do?" Matilda shrieked. "If he's balmy enough to get stuck in a headlock, he can wait for Frank to dig him out." Her stubby wings rose and fell indignantly like a hundred feather dusters coming to life.

"Maybe he can, but *I* can't," Phin snapped, turning abruptly from the group and swinging toward the salt lick in a purposeful trot. *Reindeer stuck in the fence for three days. It's positively indecent. Sure, it's been days since a sight-seer came by, but that doesn't mean we should completely let ourselves go.*

Nominally the Funny Farm was a petting zoo of sorts, and before the new interstate had been built, there had been a fairly steady stream of traffic down the two-lane country road that fronted the farm, connecting the small agricultural towns dotted along the river's tracks. The towns once had flourishing farmers' markets, Sumalee had told Phin, selling all sorts of things from locally grown honey to wicker furniture, handmade canoes to tomatoes, rutabagas to sunflowers. Families would take weekend drives from town to town, and the children always wanted to stop at the Funny Farm to see the bunnies (*If only they knew,* Phin shuddered) and the reindeer and the camel. Now most of the traffic was local, and for the locals the farm was nothing new and no reason to stop.

Phin, though he wouldn't admit it to anyone, clung to the hope that someday a family—lost, or nostalgic—would spot him and pull over.

Daddy, look! Look at the pony! Can we stop, puh-leeeeze?

Mommy, that's the prettiest pony I've ever seen! Maybe we can adopt him!

So far, it hadn't happened. But that was no reason to let the whole farm go to pieces around him. Goodness knows what people would think, especially if this time Sven gave up the ghost. *A dead reindeer moldering in the fence is hardly appropriate window dressing.* Phin snorted with disgust.

For a moment, the pony feared that Sven had indeed expired. The reindeer's opaque eyes were closed and his head was wrenched sideways at an alarming angle. Then Phin heard it again: *Siiiiigggggghhhhhh.* The sound was even more irritating up close.

"That doesn't look very comfortable, Sven," Phin said in a thin voice.

A long pause, then the reindeer's eyes fluttered open. "Oh, hello, pony. Don't mind me. Just step over my legs, please. I'm afraid I can't move entirely, but perhaps . . ." He gave a feeble flop of his long legs.

"I don't want the salt lick, Sven," Phin told him. "I'm here to get you out of the fence."

"You're very kind. It's more than I deserve. No matter. Frank will be by sooner or later and I'm sure I'll manage till then." Another sigh raked Phin's nerves.

"Come on, Sven. This is ridiculous. You can't stay like this for three days," he said firmly.

"My record, though I don't like to boast, is seven. . . ." The reindeer's eyes drooped shut. "Are you sure you wouldn't like a bit of salt? So restorative on a hot day. I was helping myself just before . . . just before . . ." Then he sighed again.

"Sven! Snap out of it!" Phin trumpeted. "You *are getting out of that fence if I have to push you out myself!*"

The reindeer's lids flew back like twin rakes that had been stepped on. "Oh my," he gulped. "Well, if you think that's best."

That was more like it.

Phin hadn't had a plan when he'd trotted over to the

lick—except to make the infernal sighing stop—and now, looking at the entangled horns, he began to have doubts that he would indeed be able to free Sven. Besides being depressed and chronically pessimistic, the reindeer was, after all, *blind,* and thus not much help in assessing the situation. *But he can hear,* Phin thought, *and if he can hear, he can follow instructions.*

Phin stepped over Sven's sprawled legs to get a better look at the problem. One of the reindeer's antlers was almost entirely through the slats of the fence, and now, with the way Sven's head was turned, it was perpendicular with the boards. The other antler had gotten involved with a section of the wire mesh with which the ragged fence line was occasionally fortified, but Phin thought that was the lesser problem.

"Okay, Sven, here's what we're going to do," Phin said. "I'm going to tell you which way to move, and you try to follow my directions. Okay?"

"Really, it seems so unnecessary. . . . I'm sure I'll be . . ."

"STOP IT," Phin whinnied. The reindeer's eyes widened again and his lips smacked shut.

"Right. Now, er, move your head up a little . . . a little more . . . now tilt it left . . . more . . ."

The reindeer sighed again, but Phin pressed forward.

"Okay. Now see if you can scoot back, but keep your head just like that."

But then an all-too-familiar yowl came from above: "Svennie, I thought you couldn't join in any reindeer games!"

"Oooooh, he must be getting ready for the Reindeer Special Olympics!" mewed Moxie, perched beside her sister on the fence.

"Are you his *trainer,* Prince Blondie? Going for *gold*?"

Without pausing to think, Phin turned around so his hindquarters faced the fence and bucked. His aim wasn't very good, but the impact of his hooves on the boards was enough to send the three cats flying off, claws scrabbling at air. Unfortunately, it also gave Sven's head a rather violent rattle.

"Sorry," Phin told the reindeer, who, of course, sighed.

It took about half an hour of painstaking direction, but finally, after a lot of near-misses and heavy breathing, Sven was free. He was also touchingly grateful, and the most loquacious Phin had ever heard him as he retold the story again and again.

". . . and then, just when I thought the situation was *utterly* hopeless, he told me to shift my weight onto my right haunch at the same time that I wiggled my head *just so,* and then, well, here I suppose I am. Not that that means much to anyone besides me, I'm sure."

"He's juhhst the smartest bay-ay-ayby ever," Wally bleated, his eyes misting fondly at Phin.

And that was how it started. After Phin had done what the farm had considered impossible—freeing a re-signed, blind reindeer from a fence—and then repeated the feat a week later, he gained a certain authority among the animals. They came to him with their problems and seemed to think he might have ideas on how to solve them. First the chickens' coop became completely untenable—the stench was making them even crazier than usual—and Phin suggested that they go on strike. They may not have signs to carry the way workers in the city had (Phin remembered all too well when the Chad-wick's grooms, led by Jack, had struck for better wages. He'd never been so dirty, but Jack had told him it was for a good cause) but when Frank showed up and all the hens were in a line outside the coop, squawking madly in his direction, he got the point.

The Funny Farm's next small drama was more nerve-racking. Early one morning, a delegate from the Fuzzy Butts approached Phin while he was watering. In a squeak that managed to be threatening despite its high register, the bunny told Phin that one of the Fuzzy Butt great-nephews had been lost since the previous night. At first Phin thought he was going to be accused of stepping on him, and he nervously prepared to defend himself, but it turned out that the Fuzzy Butts actually wanted his help. His *help*!

What on earth do I know about finding misplaced rabbits? Phin wondered. And then: *But what will they do to me if I refuse?*

With considerable misgivings, the pony agreed to look into the matter, praying that if he failed it wouldn't mean his death-by-Fuzzy-Butt. He decided to enlist Freddy's aid—given the gravity of the situation, an extra three paws and a highly sensitive nose seemed called for.

It took a bit of effort to convince Freddy to help.

"Aw, I was about to pile up z's, and now you want me to go huntin' lost Fuzzy Butts? I'm prob'ly gonna blow this joint any day now, and sniffin' dirt for mean baby bunnies is not how I wanna spend my last hours."

But Phin thought he knew better. He was beginning to suspect that beneath Freddy's tough exterior, the dog was a softie. And though he often talked of leaving the farm, here he was.

"Well, all right," he said in his most discouraged voice. "I suppose the poor little thing will survive some-how. . . . He's one of the youngest, you know. And hope-fully my punishment won't be . . . *too* terrible. Thanks anyway, Freddy." He lowered his head in his most de-jected fashion and began shuffling away, tail sunk down between his hocks.

When he heard an exasperated growl behind him, he knew he'd won.

"Heck, I guess I could smell a few bushes for you," Freddy grumbled.

But the dog did more than that. It took Freddy four hours of intense, nose-to-the-ground hunting, but just as the sun was sinking into the unseen river, he emerged from a thicket of brambles, nose bleeding, eyes watering, coat flecked with mud and dotted with thorns. In his teeth he held a small bit of gray fluff as delicately as an egg, and his eyes were sparkling with delight. He deposited the tiny, terrified bunny outside the Fuzzy Butts' hutch, barked, "Ding-dong, rabbit delivery," then retired to the shade to lick his coat and snarl at anyone who'd dare to thank him.

· · ·

"SO HOW HAVE YOU BEEN SPENDING YOUR TIME, Phineas?" The water buffalo had taken to calling Phin by his original name, and the pony found he liked it. It had a certain ring of maturity in Sumalee's sweet voice—not at all how Poppy used to bray it in frustration.

Phin eased to his side, letting the cool creek water spill over his neck and chest. His golden coat had become dull with dirt and faded by the sun, and his mane and forelock were so long and tangled that Phin felt positively barbaric. The water wouldn't restore him—Phin doubted even Jack's grooming could bring back his usual splendor—but at least it would get off the worst of the mud and soothe his mosquito bites.

"Oh, doing this and that, I suppose." Phin sighed. It had been a trying week. Wally had gotten a thorn stuck in one of his toes and had cried like the baby he thought Phin was until the pony showed him how to scrape his hoof against a fence board to free it (a Poppy trick, admittedly, but it worked). Then Freddy had actually nipped Mixie (who completely deserved it) and the three cats declared war on the dog. Everyone was on Freddy's side, of course, but then the cats had declared a strike on rat-catching until Freddy apologized, and Phin felt responsible since he'd introduced the concept in the first place. Plus, the farm was getting overrun by vermin. *I'll talk to them again tonight . . . bribe them or something. . . .*

"Sven tells me you've become quite indispensable. I see you've found more ways for a pony to be useful."

"Oh, *Sven,* he would say that." Phin rolled his eyes. "I'm not being useful . . . nobody's *useful* here–didn't you say that? I'm just trying to, I don't know, keep a little order around here."

"Because you're a herd animal, and you need to be part of a group," Sumalee said thoughtfully.

Phin bristled at that. "I *should* be around people," he snapped. "I *should* be someone's champion pony."

"But you're not," Sumalee replied, unruffled. "And so instead you're helping others. You're making the farm a better place. The animals are growing to rely on you. Perhaps you *should* be a champion pony, but I'd say you're doing a fine job just being yourself."

Phin had no answer for that. He was pleased, yet sad. Talking with Sumalee often had that effect on him.

"And you're not as fat anymore, Prince Blondie," Freddy barked from beyond the trees.

"Oh *thanks,*" Phin muttered, and he resumed wallowing.

CHAPTER 9

IN LATE AUGUST, FREDDY ALMOST MADE GOOD
on his repeated promise to leave the farm.

It was Frank's day, and Phin stood near the fence attempting to swish flies with Sven, waiting for the now
familiar sound of Frank's truck. Swishing flies with a reindeer was an exercise in futility–Sven's tail was no more
than a scraggly gray pouf at the end of his butt, and Phin's
tail barely reached the reindeer's haunch–but it passed
the time. Wally lurched over and settled in on Phin's
other side, making the irritated pony the filling in a
reindeer-camel sandwich. Wally's short, hairless tail was
no help, either, but at least he had stopped trying to eat
Phin's. Neither of his companions was a sparkling con-
versationalist, so Phin let himself drift off, thinking of the
nice spot of grass he'd found by the crick that morning.
*One thing I can say about the Funny Farm is that it teaches
you to appreciate the small . . . really small . . . things. Well,
smoke 'em if you got 'em, as Freddy would say.*

Just then, Phin heard Freddy whine, an urgent, almost pained sound. He looked over to the puddle of shade where the dog had been snoozing and saw that not only was he awake, he was positively bursting from his fur. Uneven ears cocked, straining at attention, a furrow creased deep in his brow, panting furiously: For once in his life, Freddy looked like he was going to lose his cool.

"That's a Hemi engine . . . yeah, gotta be, maybe a 'seventy. . . ." The dog sprang to his paws, wriggled under the fence, then hopped slowly toward the driveway, his feathery tail pointing straight out behind him like a retriever's.

"What's he on about?" Matilda shrilled from the water trough. Phin wondered the same thing. But before anyone could answer, Freddy was off like a Thoroughbred at the starting bell, springing down the drive and toward the road at a speed the pony couldn't believe, his wiry body straining flat to the ground.

"It's a 'Cuda! Radioactive! It's a Barracuda!" he yelped as he flew. Utterly baffled, Phin watched as Freddy streaked down the country lane, and then he heard the sound that must have set the dog off: the throaty rumble of a car engine. His ears pricked. Freddy never got this excited about Frank, so the car must be a strange one.

"What's up with Freddy?" he asked Sven.

"Oh, you know how dogs are about cars," the reindeer sighed. "Freddy lives for them."

"I've never seen him chase a car like *that* before," Phin objected.

"He has particular tastes. What does he call them, Wally? The automobiles he's so fond of?"

"Haaawt raaawds," the camel mooed.

Unenlightened, Phin resumed fly-swishing. A minute later, he spotted the car, then spotted Freddy, hot on its heels. He was still barking his head off.

"A 'Cuda! A 'Cuda! Got a dual carb! A Barracuda! Crazy!"

Phin thought *Freddy* was crazy. The car looked like an old two-door junker, and it made an unseemly racket as it tore past the farm. It certainly wasn't in the same class as the Ingrams' luxury sedan. There was just no accounting for taste.

Twenty minutes later, Freddy came panting back down the drive. He looked beat, but his eyes held a fanatical gleam.

"Couldn't . . . make 'em . . . stop," he gasped. "Too

fast . . . for this . . . tripod daddy-o. But man . . . that was one . . . unreal street machine." He collapsed in a heap in his patch of shade, sides heaving.

"Why did you want them to stop?" Phin wondered. "I mean, I get it that you like the car, but what are you going to *do* with one?"

"Catch a ride . . . out of . . . Nowheresville, hombre. I'm just . . . bidin' my time . . . waitin' for . . . the right ride." Freddy staggered to his paws and headed for the water trough.

It was a typically hot day, but Phin suddenly felt cold all over. *The farm without Freddy?* It was not a place the pony wanted to imagine. And just as he realized how much he'd miss the mutt, Phin also realized that he had a friend. He looked with real affection at the dirty, flea-bitten, three-legged dog and knew that he'd never met anyone quite like him.

"*I* didn't think that car was anything special," he said petulantly.

"Aw, Phinny, don't tell me you're dumb as a cat about cars! And here I thought you'd wised up some. Well, I'll give you a break, I guess, seein' as you can't exactly ride in one. But brother, I tell you, there ain't nothin' in the world better'n being in the bucket seat of a hot rod, nose out the window, layin' a patch of highway. . . ." Freddy's eyes glazed over dreamily, and then he was asleep.

He called me "Phinny."

. . .

JUST WHEN PHIN THOUGHT IT COULDN'T GET any hotter, it did. The air was so humid, it was like having your face pressed up against Wally's muzzle, only less stinky. Phin and Freddy spent most of their time in the crick with Sumalee. Freddy liked to fish, but he didn't care to eat his catch, which gave Phin the inspiration for a sneaky diplomatic coup. When Freddy was busy cleaning his paws, Phin pinched his nostrils to slits, picked up one of the larger trout by its tail, and cantered as fast as he could to the little barn where Mixie, Maxie, and Moxie spent most of the day sleeping on hay bales.

"Hey, girls, Freddy just caught this and asked me to bring it over. He thought you might like a change of pace from all the kibble." The sisters were still on rat-catching strike.

Watching the cats' lunch was worse than watching Sven at the salt lick, but it was worth it. Not in his wildest hopes had Phin anticipated such a complete attitude change. Even Freddy, once he'd recovered from shock, couldn't resist the worshipful, merciful silence with which

the cats now regarded him, and he took to casually tossing them his catch every day.

"Pride goeth before a fish," Sumalee chuckled. "Well
done, Phineas."

The pony was glad to receive the compliment but hap-
pier to hear the water buffalo's laugh. Sumalee had been
uncharacteristically anxious lately, watching the skies and
spending less time in the creek.

"It's the weather," she explained to Phin. "Can't you
feel it?"

Before Phin had come to the farm, weather was mostly
something he'd experienced from the window of his
climate-controlled stall, so he wasn't particularly attuned
to its variations. He knew it was hot, humid, and uncomfortable, but that was about it. He shook his head.

"Take a deep breath," Sumalee told him. "Plant your
hooves and feel the ground. Listen to the wind."

"What wind?" Phin snorted. But he did as Sumalee
instructed, flaring his pink nostrils and pricking his ears
forward, though he felt a bit silly. It was so *hot.* So hot
that it was making him jittery. *Is that normal?* he wondered. *Shouldn't I just feel lazy and stupid?* Instead, he felt
a bit on edge. The heat was all-encompassing, smother-
ing. It seemed to lay a blanket over the farm, silencing

the insects, stilling any breath of air. It was *unnaturally* still. Was that what Sumalee meant?

"It feels a little *weird.*" Phin couldn't do better than that, but it was the truth.

"I agree," Sumalee said, and the worry had returned to her voice. "I could be wrong, but it feels to me like the calm before a storm. We're approaching the season of heavy rains."

"Ugh." Phin shuddered. "I've *got* to figure out the shelter situation. The last time it rained, we *all* ran for the shed, then nobody wanted to leave, so we were stuffed in there like Isabella in her breeches. For *hours.* I think I'll assign rain stations. We'll give Wally and Sven the shed, they're the tallest, and since the truce, Freddy and I can join the cats in the hay barn. So that leaves—"

"Phineas, I think we may have more to worry about than where to shelter the Fuzzy Butts," Sumalee interrupted gently. "I think a . . . *big* storm is coming."

Her tone made Phin shiver. And like his friend, he started watching the skies.

. . .

IT TURNED OUT THAT PHIN DIDN'T HAVE TO worry about the Fuzzy Butts—at least not all of them. Despite Sumalee's ominous words, he'd decided to go forward with the shelter assignments, but when he cautiously approached the rabbits' hutch to determine its weatherproofing, the only Fuzzy Butts in residence were an ancient, lop-eared grandfather and two of the smallest youngsters, one of whom was the great-nephew that Freddy had rescued from the briar patch.

"Aw, didn't I tell you?" Freddy said when Phin asked him if he'd seen the other rabbits lately. "They took off a coupla days ago. That red-eyed goof got spooked by the weather. Said they were headin' for higher ground." The dog yawned contemptuously. "Thought he was doin' me a favor—said he owed me one for savin' that little fella's tail—told me to blow this joint and head east. I told him he was gettin' his whiskers in a knot over a pile of nothin'. Little rain never hurt no one, 'specially not Freddy."

"But they left one of their old grandpas, and that baby you saved!"

"Told you—them's some mean bunnies. Didn't want to be slowed down. Ruthless little fur balls."

Phin was now officially worried. If the Fuzzy Butts were sacrificing their weaker family members to get away from whatever weather was coming, it was definitely serious. The pony sniffed the nonexistent wind again, and this time he thought he smelled rain.

. . .

BUT WHEN IT CAME, THEY WEREN'T READY.

All day, a heavy bank of clouds had lowered toward the farm, chasing out the sun and finally kicking up the wind. The air moved in scattered gusts, tossing leaves and dirt and rattling the trees, then dying down to the dense silence that set Phin's nerves on edge. All day, the skies roiled and sulked. Sometimes the belly of a thick purple cloud would flash with lightning; sometimes the clouds would thin to a nauseous yellow-gray. The strange light gave the field an eerie incandescence that reminded Phin of the way the city park looked when the sidewalk lamps first flickered on at dusk. But still it didn't rain.

That evening, the sun didn't set so much as collapse, and it was abruptly dark. The animals gathered at their assigned rain stations—Sven, Wally, and Matilda under the three-sided shed; Freddy, Phin, and the cats in the hay barn; the chickens, goats, and leftover rabbits in the big coop. Sumalee decided to stay near the creek, though Phin wanted her to join them in the barn.

"I don't mind getting wet," the water buffalo said, smiling.

At around midnight, the heavens opened. It began with *pit pit pat pat pit pat,* like someone smacking a dozen wet tennis balls on the driveway. And then, as if a cord had been pulled, the clouds opened and started dumping their contents on the farm.

"Looks like the old man upstairs is throwin' the kitchen sink at us!" Freddy yelped.

"What?" Phin whinnied.

"I said—oh, never mind." It was impossible to be heard above the clamor of the storm.

The noise was outrageous. Phin pinned his ears back flat against his head, trying to block the rain's roar. He could just make out the sheets of water cascading from the roof of the barn; otherwise, the darkness beyond the doorway was impenetrable. Phin scooted closer to Freddy and together they faced the barn door, waiting out the storm.

Hours passed, and still the rain came down. Phin drifted in and out of a disoriented doze—sometimes the wet howl outside was Poppy's neigh, sometimes it sounded like Jack crying the day Poppy died, and then like Jack crying when he left Phin at the Funny Farm . . . Jack's tears were pooling up all around them . . . really, it was getting quite wet . . . Phin awoke with a snort, tossing his head. He was standing in water up to his cannons.

The pony whinnied in surprise. "Freddy! Freddy,

where are you? The barn's flooding! FREDDY!" he trumpeted, frantic to be heard over the rain.

If he hadn't been wet, stiff, and frightened, Phin would've laughed when he finally found the dog in the darkness of the cramped barn. Freddy had joined Mixie, Maxie, and Moxie on a hay bale and the four were curled up together, sound asleep–the very picture of a peaceable kingdom. *All we need now is a Fuzzy Butt kissing a goat and I'll be awarded the Nobel Peace Prize.* Phin gave Freddy a shove with his muzzle.

"Wake up, cat lover! IT'S FLOODING!"

Freddy jumped, sending cats flying in three different directions, and Phin heard three distinct splashes as they hit the water. Even the raging storm couldn't mute the yowls that followed.

"I'M GOING TO CHECK ON THE OTHERS!" Phin bellowed. "STAY HERE."

"NO WAY, HOMBRE. I'M COMIN' WITH," Freddy barked back. "STAY DRY, GIRLS," he told the sisters, spitting and hissing at him as they clawed their way back up the hay bale.

The rain hit the pony and the dog with a force that bowed their heads the instant they stepped out from the barn's protection. They slogged their way toward the shed, where Sven, Wally, and Matilda were huddled in a miserable, extremely damp clutch, trying to avoid the rain that penetrated the roof, floor, and open side of the leaky shed. Phin grimaced sympathetically, then he and Freddy slogged out to the coop, where the chickens, goats, and remaining Fuzzy Butts were irritatingly dry and snug.

"No room," croaked the old rabbit. "Go find your own coop." Freddy made a very rude gesture as they left.

"GOTTA CHECK ON MISS SUMALEE," he barked in Phin's ear as the pony started to trot to the barn. "BE RIGHT BACK." Just as he turned toward the field, a flash of lightning suddenly illuminated the farm, seeming to freeze fat drops of rain in place like a photograph, and casting eerie shadows over the water. The water. There was *so much* water. Phin and Freddy stood stunned as the flickering white and silver of the lightning's pale fire revealed the wave flowing up from the creek, devouring the field. Just before the image was swallowed by the night, Phin spotted Sumalee, no more than a hundred yards away. She was swimming.

"Uh-oh," Freddy said.

CHAPTER 10

FOR A MOMENT–A MOMENT THAT SEEMED TO
stretch out in an eternity of rain, rain, and more rain–
Phin's brain was frozen, stuck as fast as Sven in the
fence. *Where has all that water come from? And where is it
going?*

Then the pieces clicked into place, and Sumalee's stri-
dent bellow as she struggled toward them only served as
confirmation. "The river and the creek have flooded! We
must move to higher ground!"

"No kiddin'," Freddy growled. "Didn't take a swimmin'
buffalo to puzzle that one out." Phin knew his grouchy
tone was a poor mask for the palpable relief in the dog's
eyes as he watched his friend thrash through the last of the
flooded field to reach them.

"Where's higher ground?" Looking out over the enormous body of water that seemed to inch closer by the
minute, swallowing up swaths of the farm as it advanced,
Phin felt very small and very lost. He thought longingly
of his penthouse stall high in the city sky. . . . No flood

would ever reach him there. But this was no time for wishful thinking, the pony knew. He was long past the point of hoping that if he closed his eyes and waited long enough, he'd somehow be home again. He *was* home, for what that home was worth, and now it was time to leave . . . again.

"East," Freddy barked. "Durn Fuzzy Butts knew what they were about, I guess. Follow the county road out."

"Then I'd better go break the fence," the pony said resignedly.

· · ·

THE WEAKEST PART OF THE FENCE WAS CLOSEST to the creek and not an option—the fields in that direction were now a bleak waste of water and bracken. Instead, Phin picked a spot by the salt lick—Sven had already done considerable damage to the planks there, and while the water was knee-high on the pony and rising, he thought they could get everyone through before the flood's crest hit. A few well-aimed kicks cleared a respectable gap, and Phin plunged back through the murky dark to round up the animals.

A drenched, frightened crowd awaited him in the shed. Even Sumalee looked relieved when Phin poked his head in the door. He found that he'd grown surprisingly indifferent to the rain—the lightning was bothersome, but he rather agreed with Freddy. *A little rain never hurt no one.*

"Can everybody swim?" he asked.

Sven nodded. "Reindeer are quite strong swimmers," he said gloomily, "though of course I'll need some guidance. . . ."

Wally nodded, but then added, "What's swimming?"

Only Matilda shook her head.

Phin was relieved. "That's fine. Sven, you can hold on to my tail if necessary. Wally, you're so tall, I doubt you'll have to swim. And Matilda, you can just, er, fly. Right?"

"We're *flightless* birds, you daft Sepo*!" she squawked.

Phin momentarily forgot his more pressing worries. "What on earth is the use of a bird who can't *fly*?" he exclaimed. "No wonder they wanted to turn you into a purse!" And then he quickly ducked his head out of the shed before Matilda's powerful claws could find him. As he did, another flash of lightning lit up what was once their field. The water had gained a frightening amount of ground. Phin, realizing that this was no time to pick a fight, shouted an apology to Matilda.

"I can gun it, thank you *very* much," she snarled at

---

* Australian slang for an American. Not very nice.

him. "You don't have to worry about keeping *my* tail feathers dry. Emus run up to fifty kilometers an hour."

Oh please, Phin thought. *Like she expects us to believe* that. He caught Freddy's eye and the dog lifted a similarly skeptical eyebrow.

"Wow, that's . . . that's really impressive, Matilda." Phin thought he better butter her up for what he was about to suggest. "So, you'll carry the cats, okay?"

He had to duck his head back out of the shed as the emu exploded with indignation. He could hear violent thumps and bangs as she attempted to muscle past Sumalee to get at him.

Then: "Enough." Sumalee's voice was low but firm. "Matilda, we all need to work together. Phin's right. The cats can't swim well and your feathers will protect you from their claws. You're the only one who can carry them." Phin waited out the emu's renewed complaints and protests, straining to see the line of the floodwaters in the dark, but this time there was no lightning to give him a view. He ran through the list in his head. *Sven, Wally, Matilda, cats . . . now goats, chickens, and Fuzzy Butts.* He never doubted Sumalee and Freddy. It would be like doubting himself.

. . .

"BROTHER, YOU AIN'T LIVED TILL YOU'VE SEEN three cats riding shotgun on an emu." Freddy gave a vigorous shake as he hopped into the coop, sending a spray of water into Phin's face. The pony hardly noticed. What he *did* notice was that Freddy's spirits seemed in inverse proportions to the worsening storm. The dog had been tirelessly herding goats through the field to the gap in the fence and then to a rendezvous point on the road where Wally and Matilda and her jockeys already waited. He was winded, but his eyes positively shone with delight. He licked at his coat for a moment, then seemed to give it up as a bad job.

"Water's gettin' pretty deep by the gap, Phinny," he commented. "We better go on and get everybody out. It means swimmin'."

"I know, I know," the pony whinnied with frustration. "I just can't figure out what to do with the chickens. They're so petrified, they're just running around like, like . . . well, you know."

"Like the sky is falling?" Freddy barked with laughter. "Or like their heads were cut off?"

"*Don't get them going again! I just got them calmed down!*" Phin whickered vehemently.

"Like maybe there's a fox in the hen–" A tremendous explosion swallowed the rest of Freddy's sentence.

Dog, chickens, rabbits, and pony were thrown together in a wet heap. Phin felt his bones rattle with the impact of what could only have been a very, very close lightning strike. *Like the time the Ferris wheel was hit—the simp heister, Poppy and Jack called it—"The heister got it in the keister!" Poppy had neighed. . . . Now we're getting it in the keister.*

And then the coop collapsed around them.

"Freddy! Ouch, what was—"

Bock BOCK BOCK bock bockbockbock!

"Great jumpin' Jehosaphat . . ."

The world was very dark, very wet, and apparently upside down. Phin's nostrils were filled with muck and he wasn't entirely sure where or what he had landed on. Shards of wood and wire lay strewn around him, snaring up his legs and tail, and his eyes were bleary with mud. He was uncomfortable, especially now that he was out in the torrential downpour instead of under the protection of the defunct chicken coop, but he didn't think he was actually injured. Just as he was struggling to his hooves, shoving off various bits of wreckage, the flood's big wave reached them.

Suddenly Phin was swimming. It happened as fast as that. He whinnied with surprise, his legs uselessly thrashing beneath him. He'd never swum before, and it took him a minute to coordinate his movements. "Freddy!" he cried. "Freddy, where are you?" He couldn't see the dog anywhere, but a flicker of lightning showed him a tree branch full of chickens.

"Freddy!" he neighed again into the storm.

He heard a high whine just to his right, and Freddy surged forward to deposit the ancient Fuzzy Butt onto Phin's back. He looked dead from shock already. Freddy's head was just above water, his mouth still filled with fur. But his eyes danced with merriment.

"Shoot low, they're ridin' Shetlands," he managed out of the corner of his mouth.

"*What?*" Phin neighed.

"Never mind, Phinny—just an expression. Don't you got a blind reindeer to rescue?"

Phin had forgotten all about Sven. He swam in circles, trying to orient himself, but the world was a mad, dangerous place for a pony. Water surged around him, tossing wavelets in his eyes and twirling branches in his path. He couldn't begin to imagine where the shed had been—all he could make out of the once all-too-familiar contours of the Funny Farm was a vast expanse of lightning-dazzled water and tree branches. He scanned the branches, hoping to find Sven's antlers camouflaged among them. What was oak, what was reindeer? And then in another burst of lightning Phin spotted two swooping arcs that were far too graceful to belong to a storm-battered tree. Sumalee!

"I see them!" Phin trumpeted. "Get to the road, Freddy—we'll meet you there."

Swimming wasn't difficult, but it was tiring, and by the time Phin reached Sven and Sumalee, his hooves longed for terra firma. The reindeer and the water buffalo, both strong swimmers, were calmly plowing through the waste-strewn waters, Sumalee looking perfectly in her element, and Sven looking rather like this was how he'd always imagined his end would come. For a moment Phin wondered why he bothered to go back for them. *My herd,* he thought, remembering something that Sumalee had once said. *And what a herd it is.*

"Phineas!" Sumalee bellowed. "See, Sven, I told you he'd fetch you. He's been inconsolable," she added in a lower voice as Phin reached her side. "He said you promised to guide him and he was *quite sure* he'd never make it without you."

Sven sighed heavily.

My herd, Phin thought again.

"Well, here I am, Sven, so buck up. No, um, pun intended. When I say 'go,' open wide and start hunting around for my tail, 'kay?"

" 'Kay," Sven said.

"Go!"

It was a long, hard swim back to the fence line. Only a few posts were visible above the water, and Phin hoped hard they'd be able to swim over the remaining boards without injuring their legs. His neck was aching from the strain of keeping his head above water and his forelock was plastered over his face; luckily, Sven was being considerate about keeping slack in his tail so he wasn't too much of a drag. Sumalee had convinced the old rabbit to hop onto the top of her head, where he sat perched like a very unhappy, sodden hood ornament.

"Freddy should be just ahead," Phin neighed back to Sumalee. His words were drowned, as the world was drowned, in the unending, all-encompassing rain. Phin swam. All of his muscles ached, his head ached from the noise of the storm, his heart pounded out his worry for his friends. *I've done what I could. We'll all be together soon.* He swam, past the floating remains of the shed, past a bit of peaked roof that was the hay barn, past the decimated chicken coop. His legs flagged and his head drooped lower and lower into the water. He thought of his Poppy, carrying children whose weight he could hardly bear. He thought of Poppy, turning circle after circle with one child after another, never complaining, never fussing, never refusing. *Poppy's reward was the work. The work and Jack. Jack's friendship. Jack's respect.* His head dipped lower, water seeping into his ears. *My gutcher. My brave gutcher. That was no work for a pony, but a pony did it.* He thought of his mother and his heart nearly broke. *I wanted to make her proud. And now I want to make them all proud. As I am proud of them, Poppy and my gutcher. The ponies that work. The ponies that love.* And though he knew it was only the noise of the storm filling his waterlogged ears, he thought for a moment that he heard a sigh in the wind, a ripple in the water: *You have. They are.*

. . .

IT SEEMED LIKE A DREAM WHEN HIS HOOVES FI-nally scraped road. There had been so many false alarms: He'd kicked submerged tree limbs, planks, and other pieces of flotsam from the flood's destruction and each one had raised—and dashed—hope of *land.* But this time as Phin moved his trembling legs forward, the obstruction didn't float away. *Not an obstruction. Road.* The exhausted pony reached for his last ounce of energy and staggered on, the water now to his neck, to his chest, and finally to his knees. He stopped, flanks trembling from exertion, head bowed.

"It makes absolutely no sense that I'm thirsty, does it?" he panted.

"I think that's what they call *irony*." Even Sumalee sounded winded.

Sven's eyes were closed, but he still had a firm chomp on Phin's tail.

"Well, I'm not drinking this dreck," Phin sniffed. "Let's find the others and head for civilization."

Wally, Matilda, the cats, and the goats had had to retreat quite a ways down the road, pursued by ever-encroaching water. Phin, fending off Wally's slobbering kisses, was glad they looked none the worse for wear, though the goats, lower to the ground, were filthy. But then, everyone stank of wet and fur and mud and feathers. Only the cats, perched loftily on their feathered, albeit wet, nest, managed to preserve a certain air. The rain had finally slowed to a steady, annoying drizzle, and ahead the sky was beginning to lighten, a paler gray on gray. Phin could hardly believe it. He thought the night would last forever.

"Where's Freddy?" he asked suddenly.

No one answered.

"*Where's Freddy?*" Phin repeated. Another silence followed his question, broken, finally, by Matilda.

"Last we saw, he was going for a rabbit."

Phin stared at her. "For fun?" he said, bewildered.

"Lil bu-u-nnny gonna dro-o-wn," Wally bleated. "Fre–Fredddyyy . . ." He stopped.

Phin couldn't bear it. "WHAT? FREDDY *WHAT? WHERE IS HE?*"

"We don't know," Matilda said abruptly. "He . . . he went walkabout, didn't he? How could we tell what was happening, cats on our back, lightning everywhere, dog swimming in circles. He just . . . wasn't there anymore."

Phin's neigh echoed over the wet gray world. Tearing his tail from Sven's mouth, he forced his weary body back into the water, plunging up to his chest and throwing his legs out to swim again.

"Freddy! *FREDDY!*"

He was so tired, he could hardly keep the tip of his muzzle above the water, but Phin swam on blindly, not knowing where to go, his legs frantic pistons beneath him.

"FREDDY!"

And then someone was swimming beside him. Someone was steering him, pressing their body against his. Someone was shoving their back under his neck to support his head and was carrying him back, back to the silent group of animals, away from Freddy.

"*Freddy,*" Phin whispered, too weak to fight Sumalee as she brought him back to land.

"He'll come back," she murmured. "He always does."

. . .

THAT MORNING, A VERY STRANGE PROCESSION approached the sleepy, soggy main street of Gibsonville. At its head, a thin, ragged pony of indeterminate color plodded, head down, his long, tangled mane a veil hanging past his neck. Behind him followed a reindeer, holding the end of the pony's muddy tail in his mouth. Flanking the reindeer were a camel and a water buffalo. Riding the camel and the water buffalo were a white chicken and a lop-eared rabbit, respectively. Taking the rear were three cats astride an emu and a pack of goats.

"Wh-e-re are we?" Wally's bleat was like a lament.

Phin looked up, surveying the neat rows of cottages and gardens glistening with rain in the soft, pearly light of morning.

"Who knows?" he said dully. Everyone was quiet again.

Phin wondered vaguely what to do next. They needed food and drinking water. They needed a home. *I need Freddy.* He continued walking.

The parade of animals continued past the cottages. Suddenly the old Fuzzy Butt fell off of Sumalee's head.

I knew he wasn't going to make it, Phin thought. But to his surprise, the rabbit lurched to his paws and began hopping slowly to the sidewalk. Phin cocked his head at Sumalee, but she looked just as perplexed. The pony glanced up to the house, set back from the road, that the rabbit seemed to be hobbling toward. There was movement on the porch. Phin took a few more steps, then saw a rabbit hutch perched near the cottage's front steps. Two small bunnies appeared to be huddled inside, chewing on lettuce being handed through the bars by a young, pretty girl with blond braids. Her other hand was occupied with scratching the belly of a very dirty dog whose closed eyes and lolling tongue spoke deep contentment.

"A pony!" the little girl shouted, pointing at Phin.

The dog rolled over reluctantly and opened one eye.

"Hey, Phinny. What took you so long?" Freddy yawned.

EPILOGUE

A PHOTOGRAPH, TAKEN BY A GIBSONVILLE citizen, of Phin and the Funny Farm herd walking down Main Street was picked up by a news wire and ran in papers across the country above captions such as "Plucky Pony and Friends Survive Storm" and "No Ark Required: Animals Brave Worst Flood in Twenty Years." Frank collected all of the clippings and mounted them on the new bulletin board above the donations box at the entrance to the animals' new, old home.

It was their old home in that it stood in the same location; new, because so much had changed. After spending some time in cramped temporary housing provided by a local pig farmer (the experience made Phin *very* glad that pigs seemed, bafflingly, to be prized creatures and thus not candidates for the Funny Farm), the animals were moved back to the soggy, muddy pit that had been their home. But it didn't remain a pit for long. Phineas and his friends were famous, and as the little towns around them cleaned up and rebuilt after the storm, the people made the farm a special project and poured their energy into fixing it up. By the time the produce stands that now filled the farm's driveway were selling Halloween pumpkins, it had a new fence, painted white; a real barn with four stalls, including one for the retired racehorse who had recently joined them; a new chicken coop; and even an Information Center where Frank had filled index cards with "Fascinating Facts" about the animals. He also painted a new sign to guide the steady stream of visitors who wanted to see the animals for themselves. It read:

WELCOME TO THE FUNNY FARM / HOME OF PHINNY, THE BRAVE PONY.

Phin tried not to let it all go to his head, which wasn't difficult with Freddy and Sumalee around. But when one day Jack showed up, it was impossible to keep his happy pride in check, especially when Jack saw the sign . . . and wept.

"Phinny, my lad, my love, look at you." Jack beamed at him. "You're a right mess, but you're famous."

Phin could hardly stand still. He pranced in place and turned circles around Jack, like Freddy around a cool car.

"Freddy! Sumalee!" he whinnied. "This is Jack! Sven, Wally! Come meet my friend!"

Jack had brought a bucket of brushes, and after giving Phin a thorough shampoo and condition, the groom went to work polishing, buffing, and untangling. He picked his hooves (shoeless now, though Phin couldn't remember when he'd lost them all) and Phin didn't once lean his weight on him. The pony settled dreamily into the unexpected, almost forgotten luxury, marveling that he had once taken it for granted. He was so preoccupied with all of the nice things being done to him that at first he didn't notice the glum faces of his friends.

"Is he gonna ta-a-ake you ba-a-ack to your mo-o-o-mmy, Prince Baby?" Wally asked tremulously.

"Don't worry about *me*," Sven sighed. "I'm sure *someone* will take pity on me the next time I get stuck in the fence. Or not. I suppose it doesn't much matter."

"Good riddance!" shrieked Matilda, who still hadn't forgiven Phin for making her a cat taxi.

Just then, Jack reached in his pocket and offered Phin something from his hand. The pony took it automatically. The blast of sweetness hit his tongue, filling his mouth with a cloying, overwhelming saccharine taste. He spit it out hastily.

"Since when don't you like sugar?" Jack stared at him in bewilderment.

That was sugar? *I feel like washing my mouth out.* And then Van der Luyden's words came back to him once again: *"We endure, even without sugar." I suppose I did,* Phin thought, *and now I've lost my taste for it.* He didn't waste much time wondering about it. Giving Jack an apologetic look, he trotted back to Sven and Wally.

"I can't leave you," he said simply. "This is where I belong."

"Phinny of the Funny Farm." Sumalee winked at him.

"Righto, stay. I'll fill your berth." Freddy's voice came from farther away—a high, desperate whine. Phin looked around, and finally spotted him in the front seat of Jack's car, his face rigid with a kind of ecstatic reverence.

"What are you doing in Jack's car?" Phin neighed.

"Car? Car? You call this radioactive cherry a *car*? This is a 1967 Camaro Z28 Coupe with a 302 under the hood and a Holley 4-barrel. Zero to sixty in seven seconds. Your Jack is a *god*." Freddy looked like his eyes were about to roll up in his head.

Phin and Sumalee exchanged looks. *What* was *it with dogs and cars?*

. . .

FREDDY DIDN'T GET TO RIDE IN JACK'S CAR that day, but he did the following week, and the week after, and the week after that. Every Saturday, Jack made the trip from the city to the farm, Phin's old carnival-era saddle and bridle in his trunk. And every Saturday there was a line of kids—thin and chubby, nervous and fearless, allergic and not—standing in line in front of the donations box. Every Saturday, Jack whistled to his old friend, who trotted to the barn, picked up his feed bucket in his mouth, and brought it over to the fence, where the children filled it with carrots and apple slices (no sugar allowed), which Phin generously shared with Wally and Sven and the ex-racehorse. The children took turns brushing all the animals (except for Matilda, who insisted she didn't need it), and then finally it was their turn to ride the Shetland pony—not quite as golden, not quite as glossy, but the bravest—who carried each one with joy in his heart.

ACKNOWLEDGMENTS

IT'S NOT AN AVERAGE MOTHER THAT YOU can call and say, "I need a dictionary of the Shetland dialect and of carnival-worker slang," and she doesn't bat an eye. Stephanie Wedekind—my first and best reader, former children's librarian, research assistant extraordinaire, who has a song for every occasion—was integral to the writing of this book . . . and, for that matter, to anything I write.

Kim Tenhacken pointed me in the right direction for Australian lingo, and Jim Guida made marvelous suggestions for improving Matilda's insults. Sarajane Maki, the ultimate hot-rod mama, vetted Freddy's cars and explained carburetors in a way I actually understood, for an hour. I am grateful to the kind people at Visit Shetland (www.visitshetland.com), especially Deborah Kerr, and to Mary Blance of Shetland ForWirds, who took such care and time in looking over Poppy's dialogue. Of course, any errors of dialect, whether Australian or Shetlandic, carney or hot rod, are my own.

This book, dedicated to my darling David, is also in memory of Christopher Roberts, my Freddy.

ANNIE WEDEKIND grew up riding horses in Louisville, Kentucky. Since then, she's been in the saddle in every place she's lived, from Rhode Island to New Orleans, South Africa to New York. Her first novel for young readers, *A Horse of Her Own*, was praised by *Kirkus Reviews* as "possibly the most honest horse book since *National Velvet* . . . a champion." She lives with her family in Brooklyn, New York. www.anniewedekind.com